CAMOUFLAGE CHRISTMAS

DEEDEE LAKE
SUSAN BAGANZ

ST JOSEPH, MISSOURI USA

For more information on DeeDee Lake, visit DeeDeeLake.com

For more information on Susan Baganz, visit SusanBaganz.com

For information on the Rules of Engagement series, visit RulesofEngagementMilitaryRomance.com

Editor: Debra L. Butterfield
Cover Design: Tamara Clymer
Cover Images: Ornament - 3625217 © Rich Koele | Dreamstime.com
Background - 81935175 © Supapun Narknimitrung | Dreamstime.com

Printed in the United States of America.

DeeDee Lake and Susan M. Baganz have given us an engaging story of love, trust, and faith within a military context that connects us with the themes of determination, fear, hope and dreams as these concerns resonant within us all. A text that stands alone well by itself but has planted a seed of anticipation for the rest of the series.

— V/R, CH (MAJ) Corey R. Arnold
Fort Carson Family Life Chaplain

In gratitude to our Lord Jesus for the gift of friendship
and love we've both experienced.

"Every good thing given and every perfect gift is from above,
coming down from the Father of lights,
with whom there is no variation or shifting shadow." James 1:17

Glossary

OC	Officer candidate
OCS	Officer candidate school
PT	Physical training
PA	Physician's assistant
JROTC	Junior Reserve Officer Training Corps
PDA	Public display of affection
ACU	Army Combat Uniform
DFAC	Dining facility
Cadre	Instructors
Ruck March	March with ruck sack; heavy army backpack typically with a minimum of 60 pounds
GORE-TEX	Cold weather, water resistant uniform
Quarters	Barracks or other living spaces on a post or base

1

Fort Benning, GA
Officer Candidate School

Cadet Samantha Brooke Cooper-Sanchez awoke with a start and jumped out of her bunk. Determination coursed through her veins stronger than coffee. She took a deep breath before donning her clothing for morning exercises. "Come on, Haugh, Starkey."

"We're coming. I don't think I'll ever appreciate waking at o-four thirty," OC Simeone Haugh grumbled and stretched, moving slower than a sloth.

"Nurses and physician's assistants don't always get the luxury of sleep, and it's no different in the Army." OC Gena Starkey rose and made her bunk with military precision.

"Yeah, you've told me. Stop being so chipper at o-dark thirty in the day. It's annoying." Sarcasm dripped from Haugh's words. Starkey was a know-it-all and not the friendliest of roommates. She often flirted with the guys, but always stayed too close to carrying it too far. It was annoying.

Once they all were ready, they joined the other cadets as they rushed out of their barracks to fall into formation as Second Squad, Third Platoon, Bravo Company. OC Bernard Travis was to her left and OC Haugh to her right. Today was a ruck march. *Great.* She thought she'd endured enough of that in basic. Several weeks of that here and it was growing old fast. *Change your attitude, cadet,* she mentally scolded herself. She'd endure. She always did.

Brooke had worked hard to get college credits while in high school. She joined the National Guard and managed to obtain her R.N. certification fast. Why was she in a rush? To prove she could do it.

And to make her father proud.

She glanced to her left. Bernard gave her a brief nod and a wink. They'd been in high school together while both their fathers served on the same post. She wanted to scoff at how easy she thought this would be after being raised as a military brat. Basic was rough. Nursing school had been challenge too.

She hadn't expected Bernard to be here. He was a pleasant surprise when she first arrived. It was nice to see a friendly face. She chose to lock up her teenage crush over him. That was years ago. Even if only as a friend here, it helped the time go faster.

She stretched and tried to get warm in the darkness. The order was given to begin their march. No conversations as they all focused on the singsong cadence of the words the sergeant called out for them to repeat.

A yellow bird, with a yellow bill
He landed on my windowsill.
I coaxed him in with a piece of bread,
and then I kissed his little head!
I called the doctor the doctor said.
My dear good man this bird is dead.

Brooke grinned at the silly cadence. "Yellow Bird" was one of her favorites even if the bird died at the end.

After returning from their march, they marched to breakfast at the dining facility. She kept wanting to call it the Mess Hall, but that terminology was old. She hoped she never got caught slipping in using that term lest she get in trouble. Challenging because that was what she'd grown up knowing it as. Once they'd gone through the line for food, she sat in her usual assigned position with Bernard, Corsin, Vander-Loo, Starkey, and Haugh.

8

Brooke sighed, suddenly struck with homesickness.

"What's up? You seem preoccupied, Cooper-Sanchez," Bernard said as he shoveled food into his mouth. How could a man eat so fast?

"I'll be missing Christmas with my family this year. My parents and youngest sister are in South Korea and my other sister is busy with work and school."

"That's no fun," Cadet James Corsin said. He was a physician wanting to specialize in burn treatment. He was Bernard's roommate along with VanderLoo.

"I'm stuck here too," Bernard said before taking a drink of coffee "Ugh. I'll never get used to this sludge." He set the cup down. "My Pop's stationed overseas; Mom is in California. Too far to go in too short a time."

"The military owns you now, better get used to it. Your life is no longer yours." OC VanderLoo was also a nurse.

"I'm not complaining," Brooke protested with a shrug. "Just makes me sad."

"Cheer up. A lot of us are in the same boat. Someday you'll get Christmas with family again. Just not this year." OC Starkey was a physician's assistant like Bernard. "My family will be flying over to visit; we'll stay at a quaint motel…"

Bernard winked at Brooke again and she shook her head. What did that wink mean? Of all the people on post, she'd experienced more of life with him, but that was ages ago. He'd been two years older when they first met in high school. Getting through medical school before joining OCS took him about as much time as her accelerated path to nursing. Funny how they both were selected for OCS at the same time.

He was easy on the eyes, too, which didn't hurt.

Once the meal was over, they rose in unison to dispose of their trays and get in formation to head to platform instruction. They marched, walked, or ran, everywhere in formation.

Brooke studied hard. She was assertive in answering questions and had spent her last year at home reading anything she could get her hands on about Army leadership training, to be prepared for these months of schooling to become a commissioned officer. Her twin sister, Kobbe, was trying to get far away from anything military and had been a competitive swimmer while going to college. Kobbe wasn't as assertive as Brooke, but as the older of the two by minutes, Brooke worried about her sister.

Brooke thought about Kobbe. They were identical twins on the outside but inside, so different. Brooke was driven and a natural leader. A type-A personality. Kobbe was more laid back. A hard worker but not as driven and a little lost in finding her path. Lord, help Kobbe seek You for everything. God had a plan. Brooke could trust Him to lead them both.

Being brought back to the present, Brooke surveyed the classroom filled with soldiers all in camouflage as they attended platform instruction. Her sister might not want to ever marry a military man, but Brooke had no such qualms. She still smarted over the defection of her fiancé, Clay Morton. Sure, he was destined to perhaps be a great oral surgeon, but he decided he didn't want an Army wife. He preferred someone who would be home for him at his disposal. Even without the Army, that wasn't who Brooke could ever be. She was ambitious and proud of it. There was nothing she couldn't achieve if she worked hard enough, and while the physical and mental rigors of OCS were challenging, she was nowhere near ready to give up her dreams. Clay could find someone else for that. She yawned. Sleep was hard to come by in OCS.

It still smarted that Clay didn't find her dreams worthy enough. He'd even given her an ultimatum: Clay or the Army.

The Army won. If God wanted her to have a husband, He'd need to make it clear who that person would be. Not that she could marry now, much less date. This course took everything she had and then some, as it did for everyone else in Bravo Company. Was she even ready to consider a guy for something more serious than friendship? She had time to figure that out.

If any one of the guys here were man enough to appreciate her drive and strength, that is. What had drawn Clay became the same thing that had pushed him away. Perhaps in her desire for a perfect life, she'd overlooked the evidence that things weren't that great with Clay after all. If she'd been more focused on the relationship instead of her career, maybe she'd have realized that sooner and ended it herself. Clay had screamed something similar to her when she'd attempted to argue her way into them continuing on with their plans. Ouch. Her mother always told her relationships mattered and not to get so focused on the goals that she'd overlook people in her life. She'd obviously failed, but how could she change that for the future? Her laser focus on her goals, her control of her plan, was what had brought her here. If she let go, would she lose everything?

Perhaps it wasn't in the cards for her to be a wife and mother at all, less chance of it if the spouse were military. Oh, but he'd need to be able to understand and grasp the challenges of this life, wouldn't he?

It didn't matter. The instructor walked into the room, and she needed to focus on something other than her love life or lack thereof.

If only her heart would get the message.

Bernard frowned as he pondered Brooke's sorrow. She was normally bubbly and upbeat. Her usual drive exerted itself during class and he admired her. The woman was beautiful, strong, and sharp. He'd always admired her, but during high school when the desire to date was so fierce, he'd made a vow to honor her dad's rules not to date. He wanted Billy Cooper's approval. And there was a healthy respect for her dad, Billy's, gun collection.

Bernard didn't expect the first girl to capture his heart would be sitting and marching by his side these past weeks in OCS. It was a dream come true. Sure, they'd stayed connected over the years with a chatty email here and there, but they'd both been busy. Him finishing his degree at her school was strategic. He wasn't ready to date or settle down yet but wanted to be in her orbit. Could she be the one God had for him all along?

He worried that would be a problem until he learned that Clay had ended their engagement. It gave him hope that maybe, just maybe the dreams of a younger Bernard would become reality here at Fort Benning. Not just the dream of being a physician's assistant and an officer in the United States Army, but also find that Brooke would see him as a potential, and much better, boyfriend…and maybe husband. She'd given no indication of any attraction in the past few weeks, but he'd put a plan in motion before OCS began once he discovered she would be here—and single. Had it been an error? Would she finally see him in a fresh light? God, do You see me? Can You hear the cries of my heart? Am I on the right path?

As per usual, Brooke kept him from falling asleep in platform instruction. As they left to line up to march for dinner, he whispered a "Thanks."

She shrugged. "You'd do the same for me. We're all on the same team." She smiled at him and his heart flip-flopped. Did she have any clue how she affected him just by being her wonderful self?

After arriving back in her quarters later that day, Brooke took her freshly acquired phone and rang her twin, Kobbe.

"Hey, sis, you've finally called. Listen, I need to get to work so I can't talk long, but how are you?" Kobbe asked.

For over a month Brooke hadn't been able to call as they'd been denied their phones. When the Army owned you, they got to dictate even that. Brooke understood the reasoning, but it had been hard not being able to connect with her twin. Future deployments would be rough for them both.

"Sorry it's taken so long. I only just got my phone and tablet back. I'm fine. Working hard here. Long days, lots of learning and outdoor exercises."

"No time for fun, huh?" Kobbe asked.

Brooke shook her head and chuckled. "I spend pretty much every extra moment studying. I'm getting closer to my goal of being a commissioned officer. February can't come soon enough."

"I'm not sure I can be there for the ceremony," Kobbe said.

"I appreciate the sentiment. Mom, Dad, and Riley can't attend either but that's life."

"Any cute guys on the radar?"

"Too soon to be thinking of that," Brooke responded.

"Clay ditched you, he didn't die. It's not like you're in mourning."

"I've never been much for dating."

"Too busy working," Kobbe said.

"Like you've been?"

"I'm quitting competitive swimming. I want to finish my degree so I can get on with living. I can't catch my breath between school, swimming workouts, competition, and work to pay for it all. I'm in debt with college to begin with, and it doesn't make sense for me to continue on this path."

"I'm sad to hear that."

"I'm too old for the Olympics by the time they come around again, and I want to live, and be able to eat whatever I want."

Brooke chuckled. "And not gain a pound. You'll still be swimming?"

"Sure, and giving lessons and maybe help coaching other younger swimmers for now. We'll see."

"I'm going to miss you terribly," Brooke said.

"We can do a video chat on Christmas Eve if you're available."

"No guarantees as to what the holiday will be like here. The syllabus says were off, but you understand how tentative that is and it could change any moment. I'm not sure if we'll have classes or what not. It's not a normal forty-hour week here. It's rare we get any time off, even on the weekends."

"Keep me informed. I'll be praying for you and maybe for some handsome young officer to wipe Clay from your memory."

"Wouldn't matter. Cadets can't marry."

"You won't always be a cadet, and I'd be surprised if you were willing to jump into marriage that fast. You dated Clay for what? Five years?"

"Three before he decided to propose."

"Maybe the next guy won't be so slow."

Brooke grinned. "He can't be if he wants to keep up with me."

"Keep smiling, sister, and don't be afraid to let a little love in."

"You too, Kobbe. Love ya."

"Love ya, back."

The call disconnected and Brooke leaned back in her chair. She yawned. Tomorrow was another long day.

Haugh and Starkey entered the room. "All done?"

"Yeah. I'm exhausted. Gonna hit the sack. See you all at o-four thirty."

"Bright eyed and…I'm too tired. You know the rest," Haugh quipped.

"Both of you shut it," Starkey grumbled. She'd already climbed into her bunk and turned out the light. Miss Grumpypants was delightful.

Brooke crawled under the covers and stared at the wall. Lord, what do I want? A career or a family? Can't I have both? Help a girl out here, please? She was asleep as soon as she closed her eyes.

2

A few weeks later
December 15

Bernard spied Brooke as she emerged from her barracks to get in formation before they marched to the field for PT. He sauntered up to her. "Hey, Cooper-Sanchez. Good morning."

"Mornin', Travis," she muttered.

"Up late?"

"Why? Do I look like it?"

"No. You sound tired," his said gently. "I realize we're all exhausted, but you've always risen above it."

"Give me a little time. I'll get there," Brooke said. She paused and touched his arm with her hand. A zing traveled up his arm, and he fought to not show how it tantalized him. "Thanks for caring. I'm not sure if I told you this before, but it was a pleasant surprise to find a friend here at OCS. I'm proud of you for working hard to become a physician's assistant."

Heat rushed to his face, but it was too dark for her to notice. "I appreciate that. It was a pleasant surprise to encounter you here as well. You sure blitzed through school."

"Yeah, I figured there was no time to waste."

"Admirable."

"Maybe to some," she mumbled.

Conversation was cut off as they fell in and marched.

15

When Brooke slogged back to her room after dinner that night there was a gift bag on her bunk with a card attached.

I wish for you a special Christmas even if it isn't what you'd like.

Perhaps a trip down memory lane will make your spirit bright.

Brooke frowned. She pulled the rectangular package out and unwrapped it. It was a DVD of the old movie musical *White Christmas*. How was anyone aware it was one of her favorite Christmas movies? Her mother and her sisters would put it on in the background and sing and dance their way through setting up the Christmas tree at home. An image of her singing in the choir of their high school production of the show made her smile too. She hugged the box to her chest for a few moments before setting it on her desk.

Who sent it?

Haugh entered the room and collapsed on her bunk. "My brain hurts." Starkey followed and sat down on her bunk.

Brooke chuckled. "Did you see anyone come in here today?"

Haugh rolled to face Brooke. "No. We were out with you all day. Why?"

"This bag was on my bunk. The envelope was addressed to me."

Haugh sat up. "Really? Anyone sign it?"

"No. But the gift…it has special meaning to me. Maybe my sister planned this, but I can't figure out how she'd get it here and who would deliver it like that. We used to joke that we should have played the sisters in the movie when we did the musical at school. We even found a way to make some fake fans to whack each other with as we practiced at home. Neither of us were good enough to get that part. Funny thing is, neither of us can act, much less sing well. We did it because it would look good on our college applications. Still, a fun memory."

"So maybe it's Kobbe, but what if it's one of the male cadets?" Starkey sighed. "Making a love connection during OCS would be a sweet story to tell your kids someday."

Brooke shook her head. "Total silliness. It's not like there's much time to talk to a guy here much less date. It's only been a few months…"

"Since Clay bailed on you? You're over him by now, I'm sure. Reclaim your life and embrace someone new—umm, figuratively speaking since public displays of affection could get you disciplined." Starkey smirked as she snatched the DVD.

"Two officers marrying would be a tough life in the Army. It would be hard enough for one to be deployed, but to separate places? Even if they tried to keep you together, there are no guarantees. What happens to the kids? I'm not sure marriage will be in the cards for most of us. At least not to another officer. A civilian might be a possibility, but I've witnessed firsthand what can happen. It'd take a special kind of guy to deal with what the military life dishes out," Brooke said as Starkey tossed the DVD back to her and she caught it mid-air.

"Come on. Women do it all the time," Haugh defended. "You wouldn't be the first by any stretch and if anyone could manage an Army career as a nurse along with marriage and children, it would be you, Brooke,"

"I'm too tired to think of it." Brooke rose to her feet. "Time to go out for night field exercises. It might even rain."

"Oh, joy." Haugh and Starkey rose. They grabbed their gear and ran out to formation before being bused to some undisclosed location.

Bernard, VanderLoo, and Corsin were milling around. Cadet Gena Starkey sauntered over to them and invaded Bernard's personal space. He stepped back and she moved in tandem. Seriously? How could one woman single him out and the other be unaware and blind to his adoration of her?

"Ready for a fun evening?" Starkey asked. It was dark out with soft light from the crescent moon.

Did her eyebrows wiggle or was that a figment of his imagination?

"It's work. Something to get through and learn from, that way, when I'm on the other end, I can do what I came here to do, treat patients."

"But of course. Still, there's no reason this couldn't be fun, Bernie."

No one called him Bernie except for his mother and grandmother. His nickname in high school had been St. Bernard, because of his faith and his was willingness to help almost anyone. The other men moved away from Bernard and Starkey as they got in formation to wait. Bernard was cornered and without seeming rude, how did he get out of this? Brooke would be arriving any time soon, and he didn't want her to witness him with this grasping woman.

"Excuse me," Bernard said as he moved away to grab Corsin. "Dude, she's digging in. Help me," he whispered. Starkey was giving him suggestive looks.

"Sucks to be you. She's cute," Corsin said.

"You pursue her. She's not even a blip on my radar."

"Yeah, Cooper-Sanchez is, right?"

"What makes you say that?"

"You sit nearby at meals and try to talk to her every chance you get. I'll admit, she's cute. I'd watch out for Yanks, though. He's been creeping up to her whenever he can."

The thought of Yanks horning in on Brooke irritated Bernard as much as Starkey did. "We stick together as a squad. Cooper-Sanchez and I have been acquainted for a long time. We were in high school together and at the same graduate school before coming here."

"She's got one focus, excelling as an officer. Dude, that should be your focus too. This is not the time or place to pursue a woman. And if you were in her orbit back then, why didn't you pursue her?" Corsin asked.

"She had a boyfriend and then a fiancé. He dumped her a few months back."

"Aha. The forbidden fruit is now available, and you want first shot at a bite. If Yanks doesn't get there first."

"Eww. No. She's a believer in Christ, as am I. We share similar goals and likes. Fond memories from the past as friends. I could think of far worse things to build a relationship on."

"Doesn't hurt that she's smart and beautiful. Does she have a sister?"

"Yes. A twin who wants nothing to do with a military man, and nowhere near the same personality as Brooke."

18

"I thought her first name was Samantha?" Corsin inquired.

"It is, but that's not what her closest friends call her."

"But if anyone else calls her that? What then?" VanderLoo asked.

Bernard shrugged. "No clue. She asked me to call her that back in high school."

"She's a military brat like you?" Corsin asked.

"Yeah, her dad's a helicopter pilot."

"Interesting that she chose medicine," VanderLoo commented.

"Why? My dad's a drill sergeant. Granted he thinks being a physician's assistant, even more so in psychiatry, is a wimpy job."

"He has no idea what you've had to go through to get your degree. My parents are quite proud of me. My father was an orthopedic specialist, just not in the Army," VanderLoo said.

Bernard spied Brooke and Haugh. He nudged Corsin. "Cooper-Sanchez's roommate, Haugh, is a nurse. She's attractive. Why not go after her?"

"Nah. Remember I told you about Sarah back home? I hope she's willing to be an Army wife when I'm done, we can get hitched and see the world."

"Nice dream, harsh reality," Bernard said.

"Yet you chose this life." Corsin stretched.

"It's what I'm familiar with I guess."

"But you're going to be a commissioned officer. Hopefully, that will get you some respect from your father," VanderLoo said.

"Many enlisted personnel hate officers, and my father would put that at the top of his list of the kind of people who annoy him most, after raw recruits who can't even do a sit up."

"Cooper-Sanchez is headed our way. Maybe she's into you?" Corsin suggested.

"In my fondest dreams, besides she's next to me in formation," Bernard whispered. His heart kicked up a few notches as she neared. Even in camo she was lovely. He missed that glorious hair that she kept braided and secured under her cover.

"Good evening," Brooke said.

"Looks like rain," Bernard said. Drops began falling from the sky as they were ordered to fall in to march.

It looked to be a wet evening for them all, but Brooke still shined bright in the midst of it, a fierce determination on her face as the cadre began cadence with the Bravo Company responding.

The ugliest girl I ever saw
Came walking out of the dining hall.
I looked at her, she looked at me.
I got so scared I climbed a tree.
She must have weighed three hundred pounds.
Her knuckles dragged upon the ground.
So here I sit up in my tree,
And every night she howls at me.
Brooke yelled cadence with passion.

Face forward, Bernard. Don't give yourself away—yet.

Soaked, exhausted, and starving, Brooke thought she might catch a glimpse of Noah floating by. It was pitch dark and the rain was pouring down. It was difficult to keep on her feet while maneuvering through the unfamiliar dark and muddy woods carrying the M240 machine gun. Her arms ached hefting it along with all the other required equipment.

Brooke sloshed through the mud again as they engaged in their nighttime field exercises. It seemed Georgia had three types of weather—cold, flooding, and stinking hot the rest of the year. A yell to her right arrested her attention. Starkey had fallen in the mud.

"Get up, Starkey," Brooke ordered.

"I can't. I sprained my ankle or something." The cadet moaned.

Brooke sank to her knees in the mud next to the whimpering officer. She touched the woman's ankle and the cadet gasped in pain.

"Let's get you up and out of here."

"Where's Travis?"

"No clue. Last I noticed he was ahead of us. In case you haven't realize it, it is the middle of the night, there's no moon, and it's raining. Visibility is limited. I'm surprised I could see you. I'm what you have. Let's move." Brooke helped the woman stand and limp to the back of the line toward the Commander of Cadets. "Sir, Officer Candidate Starkey has an injury."

"Secure her and get back to your team."

"Yes, sir." Brooke settled the muddy cadet on a log and elevated the sore ankle. "Stay put."

"You can't leave me." Starkey grabbed Brooke's arm as she tried to stand.

"Orders are orders. We'll be back for you, never fear." Brooke headed back into action with her weapon at the ready. The cold damp mud now covered most of her lower body, causing her uniform to stick to her skin like glue, making every step harder. That would be fun to clean later. She was chilled to the bone. She needed to find her platoon. Gunshots were fired, and she rushed to meet with the others, hoping that Starkey's injury would be the only one that night.

OC Gregory Yanks appeared out of nowhere. He was in First Squad Second Platoon. Any time he was near, he gave her the heebie-jeebies, but he was a fellow cadet and she needed to learn to work with him.

"What are you doing here?" she hissed. She initially had aimed her gun his direction but turned it away now. Good thing her finger wasn't on the trigger.

"How are you, Cooper-Sanchez?" Yanks asked.

"Trying to survive out here like we all are. Starkey's out. Injured," she whispered.

"I'm into you. You're the hottest cadet in Bravo Company."

"Wrong time, wrong place, and wrong woman to be coming on to." She moved away running through the woods. Where was Bernard, Haugh? Anyone?

Yanks gave chase, caught up, and leaned in close to whisper in her ear. "No harm, no foul. I haven't done anything inappropriate."

Brooke didn't tear into him the way she wanted to because they had caught up with her platoon. Bernard glanced her way. She joined them, grateful that Yanks left for his platoon.

At around two in the morning, they returned to their quarters. Showers and lights out as quick as possible. Brooke had one image in her mind as she drifted to sleep, and it wasn't a comforting one. It was the image of Bernard carrying Starkey back to medical when the exercises were completed. Why that should bother her didn't make any sense.

Or did it?

3

December 16

Bernard stretched and leapt out of his bunk. Corsin, his room-mate was a little slower to follow. VanderLoo finished lacing his boots.

Before the cadre started motivating the cadets to get going, Bernard donned clean clothing and lamented the mud-spattered outfit from night exercises. Why had the cadre asked him of all people to carry Starkey back? Last night, after a mile, the cadre ordered someone else to take her since the woman wouldn't stop moaning dramatically. Granted, Bernard was a taller-than-average man, one of the reasons he appreciated the stature of Brooke who was of similar height. He didn't tower over her like he did Starkey. He hoped the injured cadet would recover quickly, lest she be forced to wait for the next class to finish her training. That would be disappointing to be sure.

Injuries could happen to anyone though. Starkey informed him Brooke had been the first to tend to her but proceeded to whine about Brooke obeying orders and returning to the exercises. Brooke had dropped back after Starkey's injury, but one image burned into his mind was Yanks' face against hers in what appeared to be an intimate moment. Several minutes later, Brooke rejoined their squad and Yanks wasn't seen again. Was there something going on between them? He wasn't fond of Yanks. The man had a temper. Brooke wasn't Bernard's to claim so why did his stomach churn at spying them together? When she'd returned, he'd been remote and professional, and she'd responded in kind.

Let it go, Bernard.

All the cadets brought their bags with muddy PT uniforms in them to dump into the truck to take to the laundry. At least he didn't need to do that chore given how filthy many of them had become. He spied Brooke and Haugh dropping theirs in too. Life in the Army. Sure, they'd pay a fee for it but better than doing it themselves.

Soon they were outside their quarters lining up for a morning march. They did a lot of marching. Today's cadence was at least humorous.

They say that in the Army, the chicken's mighty fine
One jumped off the table and started marking time
Oh Lord, I wanna go
But they won't let me go home
They say that in the Army, the coffee's mighty fine
It's good for cuts and bruises and tastes like iodine
Oh Lord, I wanna go
But they won't let me go home
They say that in the Army, the mail is so great
Today I got a letter dated 1948
Oh Lord, I wanna go
But they won't let me go home
They say that in the Army, the tents are waterproof.
You wake up in the morning and you're floating on the roof.
Oh Lord, I wanna go
But they won't let me go home

Getting in line in the dining hall was a rush. Everyone wanted their food and coffee. All Bernard wanted was to get close to Brooke. Today there had been no sign of Starkey. Maybe she had done severe injury to her ankle.

Yanks approached Brooke while she was in line and whispered in her ear. She shook her head at him, and he left. What was going on?

Once Bernard got his food, he joined his squad. Haugh was next to Brooke, and Corsin was starting to sit down. His friend glanced up and waved him over with a smile. VanderLoo was coming behind him. Maybe Corsin was going to help him? He sure hoped so.

"How is everyone this morning? Ready for some coffee that works like iodine?" Bernard asked as he placed his tray down and sat. He bent his head for a moment to pray but then glanced across the table to Brooke.

"Too bad it wouldn't help Starkey," Brooke said before she took a sip and made a face. "I keep thinking if I try hard enough, I'll learn to like this stuff. Not happening."

Bernard sipped his and grimaced. "I've had better that's for sure, but the caffeine will help me get through the day."

Brooke frowned. "I wish caffeine would help me, but it doesn't. I'm stuck with water and trying to get sleep. Guess I picked the wrong career for that."

"Why?" Haugh asked.

Brooke's mouth gaped. "Are you serious? You're asking me that? Nurses work long hours, sometimes double shifts if short-staffed and rarely get to use the bathroom."

"Oh, yeah," Haugh said as she dug into her pancakes.

"Thankfully, psychiatric PAs don't have that problem. Long hours and high demand but still leave time and the opportunity to use the restroom."

"As a male it's easier for you out on field training too," Haugh said.

"Haugh. I can't believe you said that." Brooke almost choked on her water.

"Too plain for your puritanical sensibilities? This is the Army and you're a nurse. I'm sure speaking about normal body functions is acceptable," Haugh justified.

"Perhaps doing it over breakfast isn't the best," Bernard offered. He was ashamed he'd never even considered how much more difficult certain parts of it would be for the women. Perhaps less muscle mass and upper body strength but he grudgingly admitted to himself that the opportunity to use a tree during field exercises made training easier.

Soon they were in platform instruction struggling to stay awake after a long, physical night.

Grateful to have the afternoon free. Bernard had one plan, only one. Catch up on some sleep.

Brooke dragged her body to her room. The space was quiet. Haugh slept in the near-dark room with the blinds drawn. Starkey hadn't returned. Brooke worked as quietly as possible to put her things away. She unlaced her boots and sat on the bunk. She could use a nap. A long nap.

A bag was there by her pillow. She turned on a lamp that directed light to her bunk and pulled out the envelope. On the outside, the card was identical to the one from the previous day, a sweet Christmas card but basic for all that. No text on the inside as part of the card but the sender did leave another note in the neatest printing.

I'm not a poet of Shakespeare's ilk,
Your skin as smooth as creamy milk.
But poetry by another guy,
May help you see the reason why,
My adoration for you is pure,
But will you see me? I'm not so sure.

Confusion warred with curiosity, and she rushed to pull out the wrapped package inside, although she took care undoing the paper. She didn't want to wake her roommate. She pulled out a small, leather-bound copy of William Shakespeare's sonnets. Who would have known she'd loved learning about Shakespeare's plays and poetry in school? She flipped to a page where a bookmark had been placed. Was that strategic or accidental? The bookmark had her name, Brooke, on it.

She moved the page to the light where she could read the words.

"Sonnet XVIII"

> Shall I compare thee to a summer's day?
> Thou art more lovely and more temperate:
> Rough winds do shake the darling buds of May,
> And summer's lease hath all too short a date:
> Sometime too hot the eye of heaven shines,

And often is his gold complexion dimm'd;
And every fair from fair sometime declines,
By chance, or nature's changing course, untrimm'd;
But thy eternal summer shall not fade,
Nor lose possession of that fair thou ow'st;
Nor shall Death brag thou wander'st in his shade,
When in eternal lines to time thou grow'st:
So long as men can breathe, or eyes can see,
So long lives this, and this gives life to thee."

Her sister must be doing this. Who else could it be? The clue indicated it was someone who didn't think she noticed them. Yanks was being too obvious a flirt to be the one. When had anyone dared to give her gifts so thoughtful? And write poetry?

Clay accused her of lacking feeling, but he hated *White Christmas!*

She hugged the book to her chest, moved the card and bag to the floor and stretched out on the bunk. The question wouldn't go away. Who was doing this? She was someone who liked to know the plan. Surprises usually annoyed her. But this was more of an unsettling. But maybe in a good way. She caressed the book. God, You see the one who sent this. Open my eyes to see him as well. Throw my heart open to love again if that's Your will. I'm totally out of my depth here. She'd need to mull this over later.

She couldn't help but smile that someone thought her skin was smooth and creamy. If her heart was an ice cube, as Clay insinuated during that last argument, it was starting to crack and melt.

4

December 17

Brooke stretched before making her bed, humming one of her worship songs. She always looked forward to Sundays.

"So, we've been given the choice of a party or going to chapel." Haugh grinned. "I'm up for a party, you?"

"I'm headed to chapel. Whoever heard of a party in the morning anyway? Wanna come to chapel?" Brooke asked.

"No. I'll have fun instead." OC Yolanda Xavier, their new roommate said. Starkey was on a medical hold until she recovered.

"Suit yourselves. Enjoy." Brooke put on her coat and cover and headed out into the cold. Bernard and Corsin awaited her.

"VanderLoo wanted to attend the party?"

"Yeah. I suspect he'll be in for a surprise," Bernard said as they headed to chapel.

"Why?" Corsin asked.

"Sometimes a party is a disguise for something much less pleasant," Brooke said. She glanced at Bernard who nodded his head. "At least, that's what I've heard."

"Guess we'll find out after chapel," Bernard said. "Let's jog. It'll be warmer."

Sunday morning chapel on post was refreshing. Haugh's refusal to attend rankled and worried Brooke. She wasn't close to Xavier. She prayed for both of her roommates.

The worship featured Christmas carols she'd been familiar with all her life. It was difficult to believe Christmas was about a week away. The thought saddened her. Why had she rushed to get into OCS? She should have been planning her wedding. They'd tentatively penciled in their plan for a Christmas Eve ceremony, recognizing that the cadre had the last word. It didn't matter since she wasn't going to celebrate much of any holiday this season, far away from family. A dark cloud settled over her. She'd already purchased gifts for everyone and left them with her mother. She would miss the food and the gift opening and the laughter. Dad was posted in South Korea with Mom and her sister Riley. Her sister Kobbe would be alone. It was the first time for both of them. This was the military life.

This was the life she chose. She stood straighter, squaring her shoulders back. Christmas was not a day, it was a lifestyle of gratitude to the Creator and Sustainer of her life, the One who brought her through the challenges of JROTC in high school, the National Guard, nursing school, and now here for Officer Candidate School. Basic training had been hard, but OCS took things to a different level with the mental work of all a leader needed to know.

The singing ended, and they sat down to listen to the chaplain remind them of God's overarching plan throughout history to bring the world to the moment when Christ was born, fulfilling many prophecies. What an honor and privilege to worship such an amazing God! Jesus became a child to grow and then die for her sins. She was nowhere near worthy of that kind of sacrifice, but Jesus did it for anyone who would receive the gift.

Brooke remembered Starkey not wanting her to be the one to help her initially. Was that what many people did? Turn away God's offer to rescue them because they wanted something or someone better? What could be better than eternity with Jesus? She couldn't even begin to imagine what that day would be like when she was ushered into His presence.

In the meantime, she had a task to do here, to fight for freedom and help the hurting.

Why she needed to do this in the military was sometimes baffling to others. It was what she believed she was called to do. Her purpose was here. There was challenge and satisfaction in the process, testing herself and finding she had more strength in her than she'd realized.

God was good to her. Lord, help me through these next few weeks of OCS so I can move on into a career that I pray will honor You and help others. Help me be a witness to Haugh, Xavier, and any others who don't know You. Oh, and show me who left me those two gifts? Open my eyes to see whoever is feeling overlooked. Amen.

Bernard stole glances at Brooke throughout worship and loved how she engaged in the music. She didn't have a great voice, but she sang with the same intensity with which she did everything else.

She loved God with that kind of intensity.

Would there ever be any of that passion left over for someone like him?

Time would tell.

After the service was over, they walked to the dining facility to get a late breakfast.

"Wonder how the party is going?" Brooke asked.

"Life is more than parties, and while I'm not partial to big gatherings like that, I think it's foolish to squander opportunities. Life is filled with challenges and fun is fine, but there's more to life than that." Bernard blew on his hot coffee.

Brooke agreed but was curious. "What kind of challenges?"

"We all have them. Life can be brutal at times. God has always been faithful. We're here training for war, should the worst happen, but we fight a spiritual battle as well, and we often forget that. I'm not great at that kind of training and have sadly neglected it while here."

"The battle for our hearts is ever constant and you are not alone in lacking in that kind of diligence. But as to life being brutal, neither of us is that old to have suffered a lot, but it sounds like you've endured

31

some heavy stuff."

Bernard sighed and avoided her gaze. "Let's say being a military brat can be harder on some than others."

"Oh." She didn't ask anything more. Changing the subject, they debriefed their experience from the previous evening.

"Starkey will be set back, out for the rest of this course, and recycled." Bernard took a gulp of his coffee. "You're right; this stuff is not tolerable."

"See? Someday I'll get you a cup of my favorite drink and you'll be converted."

"What is it?" Corsin asked as he sat down.

"Spiced chai latte. I wish I'd brought some with me, but I had no clue what to expect with the lodging, and to be honest, there hasn't been much time to think, much less eat or sleep or enjoy a luxury like that."

"Life in combat lacks luxuries too. Guess we get to experience that here in some ways, huh?" Corsin asked.

"Yup." Bernard surreptitiously watched Brooke. She had plaited and tucked her hair tight to her head with bobby pins. Some women cut their hair short, but he was grateful she hadn't. He'd always admired the long auburn curls even if she kept them under cover most of the time per Army protocol.

"I can't wait to head back to quarters and maybe call family," Brooke said. They all waited for the call for their squad to dispose of their trays and line up outside.

Bernard looked forward to a call as well, to his mom. It had been too long since they'd talked. He entered his room and dug out his cell phone, turning it on. He took off his boots and reclined on his bunk as he dialed.

"Hi, Mom, how are you?"

"Bernard, it's so good to hear your voice. We miss you, but we're all doing well here. How is your training going?"

At least his mother understood the reason for his passion to help the hurting. "I won't lie. It's rough. Long days, little sleep, hard work. The food is good at least, but nothing compares to your meatloaf."

His mom chuckled. "Good to hear you have a reason to come back to visit at least."

"Yeah. I'm going to miss seeing you guys at Christmas."

"We're getting together with another family who is missing people too. You remember how we used to do that in the past when your father was gone. We'll survive, but it won't be the same without you."

"Yeah. Hey, do you remember Brooke Cooper-Sanchez?"

"She was in your sister's class wasn't she?"

"Yeah. She's here in my squad. She's as beautiful as ever."

"I remember her family. She's a twin isn't she? Red-head?"

"Yes. She's a nurse. We've kept in touch over the years, but it's good to have a friend here."

"A friend or are you wanting more?"

Bernard was silent for a moment too long.

"Sweetheart, you've always known your heart, and I'll be praying for you with this woman. If she's the right one, God will make that clear."

"That's what I'm praying for, Mom. Clarity."

They spoke of other routine things before hanging up.

Bernard grinned. His father may not notice him or show he cares, but his Mom was a gift from God. She'd done her best in spite of her own challenges. He was proud of how she'd persevered. Thank you, Lord, for a godly mom.

Brooke entered her shared room to find her roommates gone, but another bag was on her bunk. How did it get in here?

She sat on her bunk and pulled the envelope out and read the card, an identical one to the previous two but the poem inside was different. She grinned as she read it. How sweet for someone to try to write poetry for her.

But who?

Strong yet soft you definitely are
To those you care about
Let this gift like love wrap you in warmth

Better than an Army coat.

Brooke pulled out the tissue paper and the squishy wrapping gave her the slightest clue. Clothing? She tore away the wrapping paper and found the softest alpaca scarf and mittens in her favorite color, emerald, not army green. She adored comfy textures and was often cold. But who could have known that? And her favorite color? She wrapped the scarf around her neck and snuggled into the warmth. The cozy fleece-lined mittens were extra warm. Too bad she couldn't wear any of that to classes or on a ruck march. The thought made her giggle.

God, who is it? Why am I being loved in this way? How was she even worthy of this? Oh, but a man who knew her this well was softening her heart day by day. She pulled the mittens off, folded the scarf, and put them in her drawer. They wouldn't get used for some time, but someday, after training, when she was off duty, she'd wear them.

Who considered her soft? It wasn't something she cultivated as a woman. Her twin was softer. Brooke liked to think she had it in her as well. As a nurse she hoped she would have compassion for her patients—and not be heartless as her ex had labeled her.

Someone thought she was soft, and she figured it was in a feminine sort of way. As a soldier she wasn't and would be insulted by the term.

Her next assignment could be in a warm climate, and she wouldn't need the scarf or mittens. It didn't matter. The gift was lovely. She had no clue who to thank for their thoughtfulness.

Haugh almost dragged herself through the door followed by Xavier.

"How was the party?" Brooke asked.

A growl emanated from the other side of the room as Haugh sat to unlace her boots. "Some party. We were scrubbing bathrooms in the barracks, on our hands and knees mind you. Hallways and walls were washed too. Interior windows except for in our rooms. I would have had far more fun going to chapel even if I slept through it. Missed breakfast but I did get some lunch finally." She collapsed on her bunk. "And here I thought we had a day off."

"Hard lesson to learn, Haugh. There are no days off in the Army." Xavier groaned and flopped onto her mattress.

5

December 18

Bernard stood waiting for the ruck march, wondering what cadence they would use this morning. Mondays were as challenging as any other day in the military. He spied Brooke striding toward him with confidence until Yanks intercepted her. Bernard frowned. The annoying cadet soon moved away, and she resumed her path. Brooke did the uniform proud. Camouflage wasn't the most flattering for anyone, and the Army wanted to wipe away any kind of distinguishing personal characteristics. Here, they were all the same. No one was more special than anyone else. Their greatest strength wasn't individual. It was as a squad, platoon, and company working toward one goal, whatever that goal was.

He was reminded of Paul's writings about the church being the body of Christ and how different members of the body might have their role, but they were all necessary and important. If one hurt, they all suffered. The same was true in the Army, but often jobs had some duplication, and more than one person was able to fill in, still, the group worked as a unit.

They were graded as a squad, platoon, or company.

They were punished as a squad, platoon, or company, depending on the infraction.

They were rewarded as a squad, platoon, or company.

Only when it came to promotion, or in this case, graduating from

OCS, were they considered an individual. The way to stand out was to be exceptional at your job and the way you led your unit. Lives could be at stake, at war or in a hospital or clinic.

Bernard was aware he wouldn't always get the privilege to serve in a hospital setting, but the Army could assign him somewhere more remote or dangerous. The needs were everywhere. A nurse didn't always have the luxury of an assignment at a stateside hospital either. Neither of their career choices were easy to begin with, but it was a noble thing to surrender the perks of a career in civilian life to serve their country in the military.

"Deep in thought?" Brooke asked.

"Yeah. Happens when my brain has a moment to itself."

"I hear ya, so much to learn. The real world seems far away while we're here. I wonder if it will be like that when we're assigned to posts somewhere else? Did my father experience that? Like living in an alternate universe?"

"Maybe. Living on post was normal life, but Dad was on a lot of deployments. You know what that means. Soldier one place and family far away. How about you?" Bernard said.

"Most of the time we were able to be there but not always. Life went on without him being a part of it. That had to be hard for him. I never actually stopped to think about it."

"Don't think too hard. You're in too deep now to back out. It is what it is."

Brooke grinned. "I guess so." She adjusted her ruck sack. "Ready to march?"

"Ready."

They fell in line and headed out in formation as the cadre called out cadence.

One mile – No Sweat
Two miles – Better yet
Three miles – Gotta run
Four miles – Just for fun
Come on – Let's go

We can go – Through the snow
We can run – To the sun
We train – In the rain.

The chill in the pre-dawn morning air kept the march moving and watching the sky light up as the sun rose was glorious. Brooke next to him was a bonus. With the rest of them, she shouted out cadence with gusto and never faltered. Yes, this was the kind of woman he wanted by his side for life.

Was he crazy?

Brooke was starving. Yanks stopped her just inside the door to the dining facility.

"Looking good, Cooper-Sanchez."

"Thanks. What do you want?" Her skinned crawled.

"To spend some time with you."

"That's not an option during OCS. I don't want to get called out. Please leave me alone."

"Not going to happen. You are a challenge I'm more than ready for."

"You're an idiot," Brooke hissed as she broke away from Yanks. He moved towards his squad; she was in the clear for now. She sat down in the dining hall and dug in almost forgetting to pray. She paused. Thank You, Lord for helping me get through this morning's march and for Bernard's company. Thank You for this food. Help me focus. Amen.

She raised her eyes to find Bernard seated next to her with his head bowed. He was a good man, and she was glad to have him for a friend. The fact that he worshipped God elevated him in her esteem. She wondered what darkness was in his past. She wished there were a way to ask, but it wasn't any of her concern.

The one hardship she'd ever suffered was Clay dumping her because she was pursuing her dreams. Maybe staying with Clay so long was an escape. They'd been comfortable, and he'd been slow in wanting to set a date. It wasn't till she'd pushed that he'd finally shown his true colors.

Yellow. A coward. What had she seen in him? She couldn't recall. He didn't possess much drive, and his laziness had been grating on her nerves for a while.

Clay was in the past, and she'd recovered from his defection faster than she'd expected. The rigors of OCS helped. Too much to do to focus on a bruised heart. Hers had not been broken by any stretch of the imagination. Maybe she'd not given her heart fully to Clay and was only invested in the fantasy of marriage and a family? Was she capable of giving her heart fully to anyone?

She considered Bernard as he wolfed down his pancakes. He caught her gaze and gave her a wink. Corsin, Haugh, Xavier, and VanderLoo were deep in conversation.

"What?" Bernard asked.

"Just thinking. I'm glad I'm here becoming a stronger me. Better. Being a part of something bigger than myself. It changes your perspective."

"It does."

Brooke glanced at the clock. "We need to run to be on time for field training."

"Done." They all picked up their trays and the rest of the squad joined them.

Why did his words, no different than most other men she was acquainted with, fill her with such warmth? Almost like having that scarf wrapped around her in a hug.

Hugging Bernard Travis would be a wonderful experience.

Stop it. No public displays of affection allowed. No PDAs. She grinned. It was a sweet thing to dream about though.

More field training after lunch seemed odd without Starkey there. She'd been more of an annoyance to Brooke as the woman was going to be working toward a PA and believed she was superior to someone who was merely a registered nurse. Funny how Bernard never lorded that over anyone. They were all here to learn and "be the best they could be."

After training and dinner, Brooke headed back to her room. Haugh was by her side, Xavier trailing behind.

"I wonder if there'll be another gift today?" Haugh asked.

"I wish I could figure out who was sending them." Brooke arrived at the door.

"I keep seeing Yanks bugging you. Perhaps him?" Xavier suggested.

"He's too self-absorbed to be worried about anyone other than himself." Brooke opened the door to their room and another, bigger gift bag sat on the bunk. "Guess that answers your first question." She removed her boots and hung her coat before settling on the bunk to pull out the envelope and card. Same card as before but a different poem.

"Read it out loud," Haugh begged as she sat across from Brooke.

"If a picture says a thousand words, or my poetry fails to enrapture, the precious image of you in my mind, no words could ever capture."

"Awww. That's sweet. What is it?" Xavier asked.

"Let's find out." Brooke pulled away the tissue paper and the wrapped box inside. Same paper as before. She tore away the paper and opened the box. "Oh, my."

Inside was a green camera bag and her name, Brooke, was embroidered on the top flap. Inside were cloths for cleaning lenses.

"A bag?" Haugh asked.

"Not many are aware that I love photography. I attended classes in high school and did a lot of photos for our yearbook. There were a few classes in college. I own an impressive single lens reflex digital camera and a bunch of cool accessories, but that's in storage. I never had a specific bag to put those things in to carry around and use."

"Brooke. Your middle name. Someone knows all your secrets." Haugh laughed.

"Yeah. A lot of people try to call me Samantha or Sam. But who is it?" These gifts had taken care and planning.

"Could it be your sister?" Xavier asked.

"She doesn't have much money right now to do something like this, and my mom is in South Korea helping Riley navigate school." She picked up the card. "Besides, 'The precious image of you in my mind, no words could ever capture,' doesn't sound like a female, does it?"

"Don't ask, don't tell. You never know." Xavier stretched out on her bunk.

"I'm not interested if that's the case," Brooke said.

"But if it were a guy?" Haugh asked.

"Depends on the man. But whoever it is, he's definitely wooing his way in."

Haugh sighed and in a high-pitched nasal voice, quoted a line from *White Christmas*, "I wish it would happen to me."

They all chuckled as Brooke cleaned up the papers and set the bag in the closet with one last touch of her name embroidered on the flap. Someone saw her. Lord, help me see who it is.

6

December 19

The temperature dropped overnight, and Bernard shivered in his Army GORE-TEX coat with the warm liner. The morning's exercises were on the field and maybe they'd all warm up fast. The wind was blustering from the north as a polar vortex or something of that sort barreled down from some obscure place like—Alaska or Canada.

Brooke and Haugh joined him, Corsin, and VanderLoo along with Xavier. They all stomped their feet to keep moving while waiting for orders. Puffs of breath hung in the air. So much for a warm December at Fort Benning, Georgia.

"Welcome to the harshness of Army life. Why am I here again?" VanderLoo whined.

"Buck up, buttercup," Brooke said. "We're all in this together."

"Tell me again that becoming an officer is in my best interest." Haugh's teeth chattered.

"Stop whining. Cooper-Sanchez is right. We are Second Squad, Third Platoon, Bravo Company. One for all and all that jazz." Bernard stuck his hands under his armpits.

"Wow. Impressive, a Broadway musical and the *Three Musketeers* all in one sentence this early in the morning. High marks for you, Travis." Brooke's grin warmed his heart. He believed he could do almost anything or endure any hardship if she were by his side.

Soon they were on the field, fighting the wind and their own fatigue as they did the exercises ordered by the cadre.

Once back at the dining facility, Yanks pulled Brooke out of line to talk to her. What was going on between the two of them? It irritated Bernard that he didn't have a clue. What would she ever see in the man?

And why couldn't she see him?

At breakfast there was silence as they ate, trying to find some warmth within from the food they consumed.

"Days like this I wish I liked coffee," Brooke grumbled.

Bernard finally got warm halfway through their morning platform instruction. Wind advisories and the cold snap weren't going to keep them from field exercises later, he soaked in the warmth while he could get it.

He glanced over toward Brooke. She was tall and thin and her shivering this morning hadn't escaped his notice. Of course, they were all cold. How would the woman do this afternoon when the weather would be no better? He worried about her, but in all honesty some of the men had less steel in them than she did.

Lord, keep her safe. And help her see me as more than just a fellow cadet or old friend. Lord, let her see me the way You do.

Yanks spoke to Brooke as she was heading into the barracks. "Cooper-Sanchez. Samantha, right?"

Brooke stopped for a moment. "Right and wrong. No one calls me that, and here in OCS I'm Cooper-Sanchez to you."

"Come on, why can't we be friends?"

"I don't want friends right now. I need fellow cadets who watch out for each other."

"I'm doing my part."

"Really? I'm freezing cold, and you're keeping me from going to my barracks."

"Just trying to be friendly."

42

"Why? Some bet you have with the other guys?"

"No…" The way he responded made her imagine he was trying to figure out if he could make that a thing.

"Bye." She slipped into the building, leaving him behind. When would he get the hint?

Brooke took as long a hot shower as she could after field exercises. Would her fingers and toes ever warm up? Troops under Washington had it much harder. At least her training wasn't at Fort McCoy in Wisconsin this time of year. Better to know how to cope though than be unprepared should she ever be in this kind of weather. At least tornadoes were rare this time of year. She dressed and headed back to her room, Haugh and Xavier by her side.

"What's that by the door?" Haugh asked.

"Another gift? Maybe they couldn't get inside this time? Interesting." Xavier stroked her chin like a character from a Sherlock Holmes movie.

Brooke picked up the package and glanced up and down the hall. Who put it there?

"I can't wait to see what it is," Xavier said.

Once inside Brooke put her toiletries away and hung her towel to dry. Her long curly red hair was still wet, so she pulled out her hair drier and diffuser.

"Wait, you're going to dry your hair before opening the gift? Haugh asked as she flipped through mail on her desk.

"Yes. It won't take long and perhaps curiosity won't kill you before I'm done. I want my hair dry before I head to mess—I mean the dining facility. I wish I could wrap myself in that scarf and mittens, but if I'm cold later I might sleep with them on."

"Nice," Haugh yelled over the sound of the drier. "Too bad they didn't include a stocking cap too, huh?"

Brooke shrugged. Her hair it didn't take long before it was dry. She braided it but didn't put it up right away. She put the drier away and smoothed a wrinkle out of her blanket. She sat and pulled out the envelope. "Same card as all the others."

"What does it say?" Xavier asked.

"Guess we'll see." Brooke opened the card and read: "Beautiful photos I'm sure you possess. If I'm not mistaken, the image of you and the one you love best has yet to be taken."

Photos. Not taken? She pulled out the rectangular gift and unwrapped it to find an 8 x 10 picture frame of carved mahogany wood. On the lower right corner of the long side in silver nickel lettering was the word *love*.

"Five golden rings…" Haugh sang out.

"What?"

"Love—whoever this is, is looking for long term, and it is the fifth gift if I'm counting correctly."

"This isn't the twelve days of Christmas. That's between Christmas and the Feast of Epiphany."

"Not in the Hallmark movies I've watched," Xavier said.

"Then they have it wrong." Brooke let her finger trail along the smooth wood.

"I still might be right though," Haugh insisted.

"That this will result in a ring? I don't even know who's sending these. The person could be creepy or obnoxious. While I'm loving the gifts and the sentiment behind them, that doesn't make a bad or mediocre man better."

"I can't envision either of those going through this much trouble to woo you. How else is a cadet to do that when there's no opportunity to date, snuggle, kiss, or hold hands?" Xavier asked.

"No clue."

"Who do you suspect?"

Brooke shrugged. "I'm clueless."

"Who do you want it to be?" Haugh asked, leaning forward to lace her boots.

Brooke set the frame aside and stared at it. Could she ever imagine being in a photo with a man who would adore her and love her for who she was? She'd thought that would be Clay until he chickened out on her. Her sister sent her an email that morning stating she learned he would marry someone else on Christmas Eve. Had he been having an affair and thought she was too much effort?

"Brooke? Earth to Brooke," Haugh said.

"Hmmm?"

"I asked you a question."

Brooke laced her boots and rose to grab her coat and cover. "I can't even begin to dream."

Everyone fell into formation and soon arrived at the dining facility. After getting their food they stood behind their chairs until Bernard, VanderLoo, and Corsin joined them along with Xavier, and they sat at the same time as a squad.

"Anyone warm yet?" VanderLoo asked.

A chorus of nos resounded.

"I told Brooke that it's too bad she can't use the scarf and mittens she got two days ago, to warm up out here," Haugh offered between bites.

"You got them two days ago? We've been stuck on post," Corsin asked.

"It's super romantic," Haugh continued. "Someone is leaving her gifts with a card and poetry."

"Really? Who?" Corsin was sitting next to Brooke and nudged her. "Yanks? I've seen him sniffing after you."

"No clue as to the identity of the gift-giver," Brooke said ignoring the rest of Corsin's comment.

"Really?" Bernard asked.

"So, anyone could claim to be the giver. I'll admit, it was me," VanderLoo said as his face turned red.

"Doubt it," Corsin said. He leaned closer to Brooke. "It was me," he whispered.

"I thought you had a girlfriend?" Was she jaded by Clay's defection that she suspected every man as being untrustworthy?

"The man who sent them would—" Haugh stopped when Brooke kicked her under the table. "Oooff. What was that for?"

"Let it be. Don't you dare share the gifts or poems with anyone." Brooke stared at Haugh.

Her roommate accepted the fact it was to be a secret and nodded. "Got it. Sorry."

Bernard focused on his food and showed only a passing interest in the conversation. Interesting. He was the man Brooke respected more than any other. Either he didn't care or...No. Not possible. She'd had a crush on him in high school, but he was two grades ahead, maybe that's why he never asked her out.

Not that her father would have let her date at that point. He'd been firm in his rules to protect his daughters.

No answers today. All she could long for was her warm scarf and mittens and snuggling under her covers for the few hours she would be in her bunk.

The platoon got into formation and marched back to the barracks, shouting another cadence. This was the way life was, day in, and day out. March, run, and grunt or shout, repeating the silly rhymes.

Oh, here we go
We're at it again
We're moving out
We're moving in
Oh, here we go
We're at it again
We're moving out, we're moving in!

Finished with their final task for the day the cadre dismissed the squads.

"At least now we can get warm," Bernard said.

Several cadets grunted goodnight and soon they dispersed. Once inside, Brooke checked her emails and responded to Kobbe.

I'm glad Clay has moved on. I feel stupid for wasting my time on him. The past few days I've been getting some gifts with poetry. No idea who is sending them. I realize Clay would never have been this creative or aware of what I liked as this person is.

Logging out she turned out her light and with her scarf wrapped around her and mittens on her hands, she slept like the dead.

7

December 20

Bernard stretched and yawned. Everything in him wanted to stay hunkered in his bunk and think about Brooke. He wished he could be a fly on the wall when she read his feeble attempts at poetry and opened the gifts he'd selected. It was sweet that she seemed to be enjoying them but was shy about mentioning them. He gathered she still hadn't figured out the sender.

That part saddened him.

"Get up or you'll be late," Corsin warned.

VanderLoo sat up, stretched, and yawned. "Umhumm."

"All right, already." Bernard rose and made his bunk with military precision and slipped into his cold-weather PT uniform. It was still blustery outside, but that wouldn't get them out of exercising in the fresh air. He glanced out the window. Lovely.

Snow.

Not a common occurrence in Georgia but he supposed it would be better than ninety-plus degree heat and tornadoes or the aftermath of a hurricane. There were worse ways to die than freezing to death.

"Really, dude. Get a grip." Corsin gave him a shove.

"Did I say that last bit out loud?"

"Yes. What's gotten into you? You've been surly since yesterday. Are you scared Cooper-Sanchez likes me more than you? Or are you afraid Yanks is worming his way into her heart?"

"Doubt it," Bernard mumbled under his breath.

"I wonder who's sending her those gifts? If I can figure them out, she'll think it was me," VanderLoo boasted.

"What if the gifts are personal and only someone who is well-acquainted with her could understand the significance?" Bernard dressed and laced his boots quickly. Speed and accuracy where key in every aspect of life in the military.

"Why would you think that?" Corsin asked.

Bernard shrugged but declined to answer the question. "Let's get out there." Dressed in their winter camo they trooped outside to find most everyone else there before them.

He jogged over to Brooke, Haugh, and Xavier as they got in formation. "Mornin."

Brooke was doing a slight jog in place with her arms folded in front of her. Yanks was walking away. "Good morning, Travis. Corsin. VanderLoo. Did you sleep tight and not let the bed bugs bite?"

"As well as anyone would expect. You?" Corsin asked.

"She was bundled up with her fluffy scarf and mittens. I'm jealous. Why doesn't anyone send me gifts like that? My favorite color is red if anyone is interested," Xavier said.

"You brought a non-regulation scarf and mittens to OCS?" Corsin asked.

"No." Brooke hissed quietly while standing at parade rest, waiting for the cadre to appear. When the commandant of the cadre, Colonel Weibe, arrived they were called to attention and saluted as one. They were always required to be sharp, but when the commandant was present everyone was crisper than usual.

They all fell into ranks to begin their run. While Bernard shouted out the cadence echo, he tried to keep his mind off the thought of Brooke snuggled up with his gift.

It didn't work. It was an image that warmed him. Would she be that receptive to a real hug in time? From him?

He hoped so. He chimed in with the rest of the platoon.

Jesse James said before he died

48

There's five things that he wanted to ride
Bicycle, tricycle, automobile
An M-1 tank and a ferris wheel
Jesse James said in his final will
He had five things that he wanted to kill
A lion, a tiger, a kangaroo
A long haired hippie, and instructor too
And if he could kill just one
He'd kill the instructor, let the hippie run

It wasn't long before all Bernard could think about was his growling stomach and how much his fingers and toes were going to hurt when they started to warm up.

After morning classes, the squad returned to the barracks to grab their ruck sacks before heading to the dining facility. Inside, Brooke found yet another bag, set on her bunk. She shook her head. She didn't have time. Did she?

"What are you doing?" Xavier asked.

"Ohhhh, a gift." Haugh bounced in anticipation.

Brooke ripped open the card, identical to the one she'd seen in the previous days and read the poem aloud. "Spicy and sweet describes you, your glorious beauty is a bonus. May sips from this mug be a hug from one, as for now a real one is *verboten*."

Wow. Whoever was sending these gifts was stupid smart with a great vocabulary.

There was something sexy about a man with a good vocabulary. Her heart warmed a little more toward her mystery man. She tore open the package to find a large green and black plaid mug and a travel mug with her preferred name on both along with a large package of powdered spiced chai. Few people were aware of her favorite drink, and this was the brand! She grabbed the scissors, cut open the package, and guesstimated how much to put in the travel mug. She'd bring that to the DFAC and get an extra warm hug inside from the drink and the thought that someone remembered this about her. Kobbe had already denied sending gifts but wanted to be in the loop as to what was going on. Fortunately, this afternoon field exercises were not taking place but there were hours of exams to complete. This would be what she needed to give her the edge before going into those.

"I'm jealous. Come on. We need to hustle." Xavier led the way out the door.

Brooke got her bag and mug and headed back to mess. Before getting her tray, she filled the travel mug with hot water and swished it around with a knife to get it mixed up. Putting the lid back on she set it on her tray and headed through the line for food. Once her tray was full, she sat in her spot at her usual table with her squad. She settled in next to Bernard.

VanderLoo pointed to her mug. "Where'd you get that?"

She shrugged and opened it to inhale the warm sugary tea. She took a tiny sip. It was still hot.

"Do they allow those here?" Corsin asked.

"Don't know. I'll put it in my ruck sack before tests."

"What's in there? Coffee?" VanderLoo inquired.

"Nope. Something much, much better." She dug into her food.

"Not alcohol is there?" Corsin asked.

Brooke shook her head.

Bernard was quiet, but was there the hint of a smile on his face?

"Ready for exams this afternoon?" Bernard asked.

"Is anyone ever ready?" Haugh responded. "I hope so. Anyone want to quiz me?"

"Not really. I want to hear my own voice giving me the correct answers when it comes time."

Haugh must have kicked him under the table given the sound he tried to stifle.

Brooke stopped eating and took a sip of her tea and sighed. Oh, yes. Finally, she'd be feeling a little warmer inside. She wasn't going to worry about tests. Sometimes being in the moment of something sweet and wonderful was a good thing too, wasn't it?

She startled herself back to awareness. Was this mystery man throwing her off her game? Threatening to skew her mission to graduate from OCS? She couldn't let that happen. This was not the time to be sentimental or get all dreamy over someone who seemed to understand her. She frowned and set her travel mug down.

"Everything OK?" Bernard whispered.

"Just letting myself get distracted by these…intrusions into my life. I can't do that. I—we all need to stay focused on our goal."

"Taking a moment to enjoy a drink of something hot and sweet, doesn't mean you are off track, Cooper-Sanchez. Enjoy the good moments when they come. Life is full of trials, tests, and sorrows. There's nothing sinful in having a moment of joy."

She turned to stare at him. "How'd you know it was sweet?"

He grinned, "You don't like the bitter of coffee, the only option left that could result in that expression of—ecstasy—must be sweet. Pure deductive reasoning." He slammed the rest of his coffee "Ready for platform instruction?"

"Yeah." Brooke sighed and finished her meal. Bernard was correct. There was nothing wrong with enjoying something. She enjoyed the sunrises, when they could view them, and would marvel at the beauty of God even as she sweated through the marches or runs. She had enjoyed the softness of the alpaca wool last night. She was elated when she scored well on an exam or activity or performed above what she'd believed she was able to do initially.

It also warmed her that Bernard noted her expression. The kindness in his eyes and that gentle smile as he glanced her way did something funny to her inside. What if…?

December 21

Brooke tried rousing OC Simone Haugh, but the woman just moaned. "You'll get us all in trouble if you don't get outside!"

"Come on, Haugh," Xavier prodded.

"Leave me alone. I'm sick."

Brooke put her hand on the Haugh's forehead. "You don't feel warm. What's wrong?"

"My stomach hurts, everything hurts."

"Haugh, get yourself to medical. Cooper-Sanchez, come on before we're late." Xavier opened the door and the two of them rushed out and to formation.

"I hope she's OK," Brooke said as they got in their assigned positions.

"Probably just shammeritis," Xavier said.

"Oh, I remember my father talking about that once. I hope not but what if it were more serious?"

"We are in the medical corps because we want to work with the brightest and the best with the top-of-the-line equipment. If she's ill, there's no better place to be than Fort Benning."

"Where's Travis?" Corsin asked.

Brooke shrugged but the answer came quick when Bernard appeared outside the platoon formation and began to call the cadence as they started their jog.

When my granny was niner zero

She came home a peacetime hero
When my granny was ninety-one
She did PT just for fun
When my granny was ninety-two
She did PT better than you
When my granny was ninety-three
She led the squadron in PT
When my granny was ninety-four
She renewed to do it some more
When my granny was ninety-five
She was the greatest sergeant major alive
When my granny was ninety-six
She did PT just for kicks
When my granny was ninety-seven
She up and died and she went to heaven
She met Saint Peter at the Pearly Gate
Saint Pete said "Granny, you are late!"
Then he said with a big wide grin
"Get down, Granny, and knock out ten."
She knocked them out then did some more
Said "I'm proud to join the Medical Corps."

The run seemed to go by fast, but it was odd to not have Bernard by her side throughout. And Haugh missing on the other side. She admired Bernard as he led the platoon. It was an honor that he was chosen to do this. Someday soon she'd have the opportunity. The thought terrified and thrilled her.

They marched on into breakfast and sat at their usual table.

"Nice job, Travis. Is your granny still alive?" Xavier asked.

"One is, the other one is gone," Bernard answered as he ate.

At least the food was good here. Even so, with eating more than normal, Brooke had lost weight. Bernard had also thinned out more, not that he needed it.

Yanks approached her outside the door to their platform instruction. "Cooper-Sanchez. You looked good out there this morning."

"Eyes in the back of your head, Yanks? You realize we're all cadets and not to be distinguishable. If I'm standing out that much, it's not a compliment."

"Girl, you need to give me a chance here. I'm trying…" Yanks pleaded as he surveyed the cadets around them.

"Looking to make sure the right people witness this? I'm not interested. Please, leave me alone." She walked into the room to join her squad.

Platform instruction was as boring as usual. When Bernard struggled to stay awake, Brooke would nudge him. *Sleep with your eyes open* was the motto for this. She couldn't do it herself, though, and obviously neither could Bernard.

The cold blustery air helped to wake them as they marched back to the dining facility for lunch. Brooke had her mug inside her ruck sack, ready to go to fill with hot water. She enjoyed every sip. It really was like a hug. The squad was quieter today. She wished she could check on Haugh but couldn't. She hoped whatever illness she had wasn't serious—or contagious.

After field exercises in the brutal cold and another meal at the dining facility, Brooke was ready to drop. Soon the squad marched back in a more subdued cadence, and they separated to their barracks.

Xavier stopped at the bathroom and Brooke went to their room. Haugh was still asleep. Brooke tiptoed over to check her. No fever. Steady pulse. And the woman hadn't eaten all day. She turned on the small lamp by her bunk and found another gift bag there. She was tempted to set it aside, but if someone were going through this much trouble to give her a gift, the least she could do was open it.

Same card but new poem. The rhyming on these weren't always great but somehow that endeared her toward her mystery man even more.

Pen your memories on these pages,
Fill them with dreams and prayers.
You are in my heart always,
Maybe someday I'll be in yours.

Not quite a full rhyme meter but sweet, nonetheless. With delicate care she unwrapped the package to find an emerald hued leather journal with embossed flowers, gold leaf, and a fancy gold pen, with the name Brooke engraved on it.

She opened the pages of the journal. Had he written anything there? Disappointment washed over her. She clicked the pen open and inscribed her name on the inside page and then on the next one wrote the date and her location and a short entry.

Fort Benning, GA OCS

Dear Lord,

I've ignored You much during this training, and it's not because I don't want to be close to You. Help me seek You and radiate Your glory as I go about OCS. Help me to pray and seek You more throughout my day.

Bless the giver of this gift with Your peace and grace, and if he is someone You have planned for me, for good, not ill, make that clear when he reveals himself. Thank You for these gifts and the giver.

And more importantly, thank You for Jesus who is with me always and amen.

I love You,

Brooke

Bernard collapsed on his bunk. Corsin was talking.

"I wonder who is sending Cooper-Sanchez gifts? Yanks? She's a bit of a firecracker. I'm not sure even I'd be man for enough her."

VanderLoo answered. "Someone is either being brave or stupid—or both. I wouldn't want to mess with her as lovely as she is. What do you think, Travis?"

"I think we need our rest. Get some sleep, guys. Tomorrow is going to be another brutal day." He turned off his light and rolled over.

"'Night," the men chorused.

Bernard closed his eyes. Lord, You understand my hopes and dreams, my fears and weaknesses, more than anyone. The more I go through this side by side with Brooke, the more I long for her to see me. Admire me. Maybe even want me. I only want that if it's Your will.

There's just a few days and a few gifts left. If she is part of Your will for me, give me the courage and wisdom to push forward. If not, make it clear that I'm to stop. Help me to seek Your will first, not my own.

With a final sigh, he was asleep.

December 22

Bernard rolled over and stared at the ceiling. It was Friday already? Christmas was almost here and he and Brooke would be staying on post as would a few other cadets. It would be nice to sleep in a little but expected he'd still be getting up anyway out of habit. Maybe he and some of the others would continue their morning routine, but not as brutal perhaps as with a cadre leading them. It was a thought. He tied his boots in the dark, and there wasn't any talk among the men today. Corsin and VanderLoo were scheduled to fly out tomorrow.

They met the rest of their squad outside and lined up in formation. No one was saying much. Perhaps being the last day before people left made it harder. Those leaving were thinking ahead to their plans and those staying didn't have much to be excited about.

Except for him.

Nervous anticipation would best describe what he was experiencing, and it wasn't from the cold or the exercises they were heading out to do. For sure, today would consist of lots of push-ups, sit-ups, and maybe an obstacle course.

As they jogged in formation to another cadence, Bernard enjoyed making steam circles in the freezing morning air. Soon Brooke was joining in as they shouted.

Here we go again

Same old stuff again
Marching down the avenue
Forty-five more days and we'll be through
I'll be sad and so will you.
Cadre: *Am I right or wrong?*
Cadets: *You're right!*
Cadre: *Are we weak or strong?*
Cadets: *We're strong!*
Cadre: *Sound off.*
Cadets: *ONE, TWO.*
Cadre: *Sound off.*
Cadets: *THREE, FOUR.*
Cadre: *Rip it on down.*
Cadets: *ONE, TWO, THREE, FOUR, ONE, TWO - THREE FOUR!*

PT was going great until someone decided to sing "Grandma Got Run Over by a Reindeer" while going through tires and soon several other cadets joined in.

Bernard groaned. Brooke's eyes were wide, and her lips formed an O. She understood.

They were all in trouble.

The cadre shut the singing down and as soon as exercise was over and they were back in formation, he informed them of their punishment.

All for one, one for all.

Bravo Company was in for a Saturday of hard labor. Not everyone was in the same boat. Fortunately, or unfortunately, Third Platoon was assigned to work in the laundry. First platoon, which included the singers, would spend the day in the kitchen, cooking and cleaning. Peeling potatoes and scrubbing the floors…with toothbrushes. Second Platoon would be washing the military vehicles…by hand. In the cold. Everyone had assignments and no one was happy about any of it. Especially those who hoped to leave on Saturday. If they were able to leave at all, they wouldn't be able to until Sunday, Christmas Eve.

That would be unless someone else erred terribly, then they could lose their leave completely.

Breakfast at the dining facility was subdued for Bravo Company. In their platform instruction the teacher cracked down hard on anyone who started to doze off. Some cadets moved to the back of the room to stand at-ease in hopes of staying awake. Anyone found going to sleep went there. Happily, Brooke kept Bernard in line with her slight kicks when he would start to doze. How did she manage to stay awake? She didn't even drink coffee. She usually chose to enjoy her chai with lunch before shoving it back in her ruck sack for field exercises.

The afternoon was brutal. It was as if all the instructors conspired to make the cadets final day before the Christmas leave miserable and memorable.

And muddy.

Wouldn't working the laundry be extra special then?

He paused. His attitude was wrong. There were people who worked in the laundry as their regular assignment. At least they'd be warm. And Brooke would be there.

She stumbled and he caught her, pulling her back from tumbling down a ravine.

"Thanks, Travis."

"Anytime. I think this morning's infraction has us all a little rattled."

"Yeah."

Eventually they were back at the dining facility, worn out and ravenous. The quiet among Bravo Company remained quiet. Some Alpha Company started humming the song that got them all in trouble but stopped quickly lest they also find themselves punished. Everyone was aware of the infraction.

They returned to the barracks in formation and headed to their own rooms.

Bernard reclined in his bunk. His roommates snored a rhythm he could sing a cadence to. His mind wouldn't shut off. Why was Yanks hanging around Brooke every chance he got? Did she like the guy? Should he be worried? The man was strong, tall as Bernard, and appeared charismatic. He'd noticed him talking with other women in the previous weeks but hadn't paid much attention until the man set his sights on Brooke. It bothered him. A lot. He rolled over and punched his pillow almost wishing it was Yanks' face. Slapping that typical smirk off would relieve some of his anxiety if it wouldn't land him in trouble.

Was he wasting his time with the gifts? It was too late to stop now, except for perhaps the last one. Time was short, and he prayed he'd made the right choice in her. If she rejected him, the next few weeks would be awkward to say the least. He would compartmentalize and get the jobs done and treat her with respect.

To be honest, that would be easier than controlling himself from wanting to touch her, hug her, or perhaps even kiss her. His aunt had called him fuzzy headed, even as she agreed to help him with the gift delivery. Every smile Brooke cast his way gave him hope. He was crazy about her. Had been for years. Whether she accepted him or not he'd be the man his father wanted him to be and control himself. If she was even remotely receptive to his adoration of her, there would be time later for expressions of that. Just not here as a cadet. He wouldn't do anything that might jeopardize either of them making it to the end and graduating.

He wondered if Brooke would like the gift she received today. He drifted to sleep with a head full of dreams of holding her in his arms.

Working laundry wouldn't be a hardship. Brooke understood what it took to keep PT uniforms clean and the ACU ones starched and pressed. The slump of Haugh's and Xavier's shoulders indicated the deep disappointment at their postponed holiday. Traveling on Christmas Eve wasn't ideal, but they could still get home.

Entering their room, Haugh flipped the light on.

Another bag was on Brooke's bunk. She hung up her coat. Sitting, she removed her boots and set them aside. They'd need some serious cleaning tonight before heading to laundry in the morning.

She pulled out the card, identical to all the others with the simple words *Merry Christmas* on the front.

"We've had a grueling day. You'd better read it aloud," Xavier said as she flopped on her bunk.

"Fine. Here goes. 'Sweeter than chocolate you are to me, although your lips I've never tasted. Your mouth speaks encouragement to all, and the love is never wasted.'" Ohhh, was this what she thought it was? Excitement bubbled up inside of her.

"Hurry! Open it!" Haugh insisted.

Brooke grasped the box and with a small shake she heard movement and a slight paper sound. She grinned as she ripped it open. It was a gift box from Sees Chocolates a favorite from California—toffee-ettes, Victorian toffee, and white mint truffles. She tossed one in her mouth and took a bite. Oh, someone did know the way to her heart!

"Are you going to share?" Haugh asked with a puppy-dog gaze.

"Sure. I'm warning you these are some of the best chocolates you'll ever taste. And not a word to the rest of the barracks. I'm not sharing with everyone." They sat there each savoring the delicious treat. She'd try to make these last for sure. Her roommates left, and she scurried to find a place to hide her gift. The camera case tucked up high in the closet was ideal for now.

Who was doing this? After a long grueling day, she was almost too tired to think. She went to get a shower, dried her hair, and curled up on her bunk with her new journal and pen.

Dear Lord,

It was a challenging day to say the least, and the entire company was punished. I guess that's why You let the sin of Adam and Eve fall on all of us, because we are all guilty to some degree of the same sin of thinking we know better than You. Pride. Self-absorbed humans hate to look beyond themselves. Yet You called us as Your followers to be an army for You, doing our best with Your enabling, to surrender our will to Your purpose and plan. Often, I lose sight of that, and I confess my own naval-gazing tendencies. Even as I'm here, it is about the whole working toward a cause, a mission.

And my primary mission is to worship and adore You and submit and follow You, wherever, whenever, however You choose. As hard as it is to do this in the Army, I've not trained with as much fervor toward obeying You. Help me grow in that, even while I'm here, Lord. Let my life and light show You to all around me.

I received another gift—my favorite chocolates! Yum. Please help me see who is being sweet to me. And make it clear if this is someone I should be open to perhaps dating. It's weird to be thinking of that when Clay is getting married in two days, the day we had originally planned to wed. He's moving on. There's no reason for me to remain stuck. I want that if it's Your will and someone who is as devoted to You as much—or even more than I am. I hope I'm ready—that I've grown enough to be worthy of such a gift.

I love You, Brooke

She set the journal aside as her roommates returned to prepare to turn in for the night. She turned off her pinpoint light and rolled over. Tomorrow would come too soon, and she'd have a long day in laundry with her squad. Misery loves company, huh?

10

December 23

Up and ready but not for PT today. Bernard waited outside for the rest of the squad. He jogged in place. They'd be on their feet all day doing a different kind of exercise, but one thing the Army did well was keep its cadets fit. They'd get an early meal at the dining facility before marching to the laundry facility. He wasn't looking forward to it, but this was the way it worked in the military.

Soon Corsin, VanderLoo, Haugh, Xavier, and Brooke were with them, and they fell in formation as a squad to head to the dining facility. Yanks was waiting for Brooke. Bernard frowned at the imposition and stayed by her side.

"Dude, let me have a few words with Cooper-Sanchez," Yanks said.

"It's OK, Travis. I'll be in shortly."

Begrudgingly he stepped inside. Everyone was subdued. He wondered what kind of hazing the guys who caused the extra discipline had received. It would continue today, but they weren't in their squad so it wouldn't impact them as much.

A quiet breakfast and soon they were marching to the laundry facility and got to work.

After a brief orientation to their tasks, they were split into teams. Bernard and Brooke were assigned to do washing, drying, and folding. He admired her positive attitude and how she silently appeared to challenge herself to do the job with speed and efficiency. He struggled to keep up but soon adopted her rhythm and worked in sync with her. The morning flew by and while his back, arms, and feet were starting to complain about the unusual exercise, his heart was enjoying every moment with the woman of his dreams.

After a quick lunch in the dining facility, Second Squad returned to laundry. Everyone remained focused as they went about their tasks to help the regular laundry personnel. Brooke was working alongside Bernard as they unloaded and tracked the laundry and put items in the washers and driers. They folded sheets and blankets to be returned that afternoon to the cadets and other military personnel who had sent them in. At least they weren't doing the dry cleaning, pressing, or mending, which was a special skill set. Corsin and VanderLoo had been helping with pickup and delivery, in and out of the cold. Brooke didn't envy them. Haugh and Xavier were doing a deep clean of the entire area, from the floors to the machines.

This was the first time since arriving at Fort Benning where she'd been working with her coat off. The room was comfortable except for being around the large driers. Folding large pieces with precision caused her to sweat.

She enjoyed how good it felt to work with Bernard. Not a lot of conversation as they focused on the task to do them with excellence.

The cadre entered toward the end of the day.

"Travis and Cooper-Sanchez, I received good reports about your work ethic. When you finish here you are free to go. There's a movie tonight if you want to enjoy yourselves."

"Yes, sir." They hurried to finish their task while the cadre spoke with the other members of their squad.

"Do you think everyone will leave tonight or tomorrow?" she asked.

"I doubt any of them got flights or planned to leave. They didn't have permission to consider themselves released until now depending on their performances. Nice job by the way," Bernard said.

"Maybe I'll see if Haugh and Xavier will join us for chapel tomorrow morning before they depart."

"Good idea. I'll ask the guys."

"Are you going to the movie tonight?" Brooke asked.

"What's playing?"

"Not sure but I think it will be some old Christmas movie. *It's a Wonderful Life* or something like that."

Travis chuckled.

"What?" she asked.

"Our luck it will be *Rudolph the Red-nosed Reindeer* or *Frosty the Snowman*."

"I loved those when I was a kid." Brooke grinned.

"Me too."

She placed the last page of documentation of their work on the pile and donned her coat. It might be warm in here, from the laundry or the company—or both, but it was still windy and cold outside.

"Merry Christmas!" She cheerfully called to the regular workers who would have the next two days off. It was a heavier workload today and being there made it go faster. At least she hoped so.

"Are you like this naturally or are you intentional about seeking to put a smile on everyone's face?" Bernard asked.

"I'm not as intentional as I wish, but I've been praying about how to shine for God in my everyday life here at Fort Benning. It's easy to get caught up in all we have going on to forget about Him. Not that normal life doesn't make that difficult, but I'm praying about how to do that better. Thanks for noticing."

"I'd say that today, God answered those prayers. Working with you made the day almost a pleasure."

"Better than field exercises?"

"A hundred times better." Bernard grinned and somehow it warmed her even more.

They fell into formation as a squad and marched back to the dining facility where other squads and platoons were returning. Once inside they got their food and sat to eat.

"I think my old man will pick me up o-dark thirty tomorrow morning," Corsin said.

"So even on a holiday you can't sleep in, huh?" Haugh asked.

"Nah, but it's a four-hour drive home. I'll be sleeping in the car."

"A cadet can sleep anywhere," Xavier commented.

"True," Haugh said. "I'll be getting to the airport tomorrow morning to figure out if I can get the flight I wanted. I missed the one I was supposed to take this afternoon, and I didn't get through to my family to inform them I wouldn't be there at the airport. They're probably worried about me."

"I hope it works out," Brooke said.

"I can share a taxi with you to the airport. My flight wasn't scheduled till morning. I'm good. Nothing got messed up for me," Vander-Loo offered.

"Great. Thanks. What time?"

The rest were making their arrangements as Bernard and Brooke listened in silence. Brooke was grateful her friends would be able to enjoy leave with family, but it amplified her own gaping hole of not being with her own. She anticipated a video call with her parents and younger sister later tomorrow since it would already be Christmas morning for them.

Once they were finished, they jogged back to their barracks.

"See you later?" Bernard asked.

"Sure. Why not? No other reindeer games on the schedule." She grinned as they parted, and she followed Haugh and Xavier toward their barracks.

Yanks stepped out of the shadows. "Cooper-Sanchez."

"Go ahead. I'll catch up in a second," Brooke said. She turned to Yanks. "I don't understand what your deal is, but this needs to stop. I told you repeatedly that I'm not interested in you as any more than a fellow cadet."

"Awww, come on, Samantha. You're passionate and I want that directed to me." He gripped her wrist hard and tried to pull her close. Thankfully, her father prepared her for men like this. She moved and flipped him on his back on the cold ground. He stayed sprawled there, gasping for air.

"You got a taste of my passion. Do you want more?" Brooke ground out, wary he might suddenly attack again.

The commandant of the cadets, Colonel Weibe, rushed over. "Cooper-Sanchez, what's going on here?"

Haugh and Xavier, who had waited inside the doors, now rushed out.

"Sir, he snatched her," Haugh stated.

"I witnessed it, too, sir. He's been bothering her all week," Xavier said.

"Get up, Yanks. What do you have to say for yourself?" Colonel Weibe asked.

Brooke stepped aside as the Colonel Weibe pulled Yanks to his feet.

"She hurt me," Yanks whined.

"Testimony of three cadets indicate you were the one acting inappropriately." He turned to Brooke. "Let's go. We have a zero-tolerance policy and Cadet Yanks you're done."

"Yes, sir." Brooke and Yanks said in unison.

"Come with me. We'll get this taken care of quickly." The Commander of Cadets seized Yanks and ordered, "March." Calling out a cadence as Brooke followed behind.

Paperwork was quick and she scurried back to the barracks. She didn't want to cause trouble for Yanks, but he had been getting pushier. The way he tried to grab her like he did could be a sign of worse things to come. Her father would be proud.

She entered the barracks and headed to her quarters. Several cadets peeked out their doors.

"Did you really flip Yanks?" one asked.

"Yes."

She finally made it behind her own door to find Haugh and Xavier waiting.

"I'm proud of you. Way to go. Who taught you those moves?" Xavier said.

"My father. Three teenage girls? He wanted us prepared. Never needed to use it till now."

"What do you think will happen to him?" Haugh asked.

"Disciplined or released from active duty due to behavior unbecoming an officer," Xavier said.

"Unfortunately, it will be the latter, he will wash out of the course since this has been going on for a while," Brooke said.

"Do you feel bad for reporting him?"

"Absolutely not. Why should I? He was inappropriate. You were witnesses. Commandant was close enough to witness it. I won't apologize for defending myself."

"What if he was the one sending the gifts?" Xavier inquired.

"Doubt it. He was too into himself and didn't even understand that I like to be called Brooke, not Samantha." She changed the subject. "Either of you coming to the movie tonight?" Brooke asked. After all that happened, she wasn't sure she wanted to go. People would be talking.

"Nah. I'm tired and want my sleep. I'll shower, pack, and hit the sack. Early morning if I'm going to find a flight out. I'll spend my day at the airport on standby. It'll be worth it to see my family." Haugh put her suitcase on her bunk.

Xavier had already started packing hers. "I'll pass. I'd rather sleep."

Brooke stopped by her bunk. Another gift? This was number nine. She pulled out the card and opened it to read:

An officer and soldier to your very core.

But first of all, a woman I long to adore.

Whoa. Brooke fanned herself with the card. This had better not be from Yanks.

"Spill," Haugh said.

Brooke handed her the card to read for herself. She sat on her bunk and pulled a wrapped package out of the box, same paper as all the others. She gently unwrapped it and in the box with a clear window to it was an exquisitely constructed nutcracker in a camouflage uniform. She opened the top of the package and pulled him out and held him gently.

"A nutcracker?" Xavier asked.

"Are you familiar with the story behind the ballet?" Brooke asked.

"No." Xavier sat on her bunk, waiting with eyes wide open almost like a kid on Christmas morning.

"The young girl gets a nutcracker on Christmas Eve—a soldier. He gets broken and fixed. She needs to go to bed but sneaks down to the room and holds the nutcracker and goes to sleep with him in her arms. She has terrible dreams where the nutcracker fights the Mouse prince. She helps save the Nutcracker and they travel to the land of sweets to meet the Sugar Plum Fairy and the little girl is in love."

"But she wakes up and he's still a simple painted piece of wood," Haugh scoffed.

"It's a lovely tale. Maybe I'll watch it sometime," Xavier said softly.

"It is. The music and dancing are enchanting. The words of the poem and the sentiment behind this gift is, like, wow." Brooke wiped away a tear. "I hope I discover who my mystery man is soon. He might not like it if I transfer all my affection to this guy." She chuckled and the gals joined in.

"At least this one is low maintenance," Haugh quipped.

Brooke placed him on the dresser by her bunk but saved the box to store him in later. At least over break she could enjoy her nutcracker prince while waiting for the real one to reveal himself.

How much longer would it be?

Bernard waited outside the barracks for Brooke to arrive. The news about Yanks had already filtered through the company. The man was not returning to OCS if he assaulted another cadet. He wondered how Brooke was holding up. Had she been injured?

The movie would be starting soon, and it was a few blocks away. He shivered. Had she received his gift? Did she like it? An involuntary shiver overtook him from fear instead of the cold as he considered how he would deliver the last one tomorrow. Would she reject him once she figured out it was him? Or would she grant him the favor of at least giving them a solid chance?

Brooke emerged from the building and put on her cover.

"Shall we?" he asked.

"Yes."

"The rest aren't coming?"

"No. Shower, pack, and sleep. They can't wait to get out of here tomorrow morning. Same for Corsin and VanderLoo I expect?"

"Bingo. I'm sad that some of their plans got messed up. While having a light day would have been nice today, I'm glad I got to spend it with you. Definitely made it more pleasurable." He stared straight ahead and kept his hands in his pockets to keep warm.

"Ditto. Grueling work but good. I'll appreciate the laundry service a lot more than I did before."

Bernard chuckled. "Ditto." He pulled the door open to the post theater and allowed her to enter first. Once inside they got some popcorn and soda and found a spot to sit. With a lot of soldiers going home for Christmas, they had plenty of seating options.

"You're not going to ask?" Brooke took a bite of her popcorn.

"Ask what?"

"About Yanks? Come on, I'm sure the tale spread to every company, not just Bravo."

"Did he hurt you?"

"He annoyed me and wouldn't stop pestering me. He gripped my wrist too hard; it wasn't a loving gentle grab. I flipped him and the Commander of Cadets witnessed it. I wrote a report. He will be washed out of the course. His behavior was the final nail in the coffin of his opportunity to become an officer. End of story."

"Did that shake you up?" Bernard had no sympathy for Yanks because every cadet understood the rules about public displays of affection. Although, this wasn't affection. And they knew sexual misconduct was never tolerated.

"A little. A few deep breaths and some time with Haugh and Zavier and I'm ready to put it behind me and enjoy a good movie with a friend."

A friend. His heart sank. She viewed him as a friend. He didn't dare ask for more especially after the business with Yanks. Would she ever consider him for more than that?

"Bernard, did you ask what the movie was?" Brooke asked.

"Nah. I wanted to be surprised."

The theater darkened and the National Anthem began playing. Everyone stood to honor flag, country, and duty.

The movie began. Seriously? *White Christmas*? But of course. Why wouldn't it be? The story starts in the Army, and they refer to the Army throughout. She relaxed as a tear escaped.

"Are you OK?" Bernard asked.

"Yes. I'm wonderful. In fact, I'm great. I didn't think I would be after the business earlier. This has turned out to be a sweet time."

His teeth shone in the dark, indicating a smile. "Glad to hear. I concur."

Some of the audience sung along to some of the songs especially at the end. When the lights came on and they turned to exit, they found a light snow falling.

She walked beside Bernard back to the barracks, wishing she could be holding his hand. Tonight was as close to a date a cadet could get as touching was off limits while in uniform. She sighed. What if Bernard was her gift-giver?

But what if he wasn't?

They reached the barracks. "Good night," Bernard said. "Sweet dreams."

The image of the nutcracker sitting on here dresser brought a smile to her face. "Good night, Bernard. Sweet dreams to you."

She went to her room and snuck in as her roommates dozed. She undressed and snuggled into her bunk, dreaming of nutcracker princes and sweet sugar kisses.

11

December 24

Brooke awoke to find her roommates already gone. She had slept like a baby and stretched with a grin on her face. She spied the nutcracker on the dresser. Leave had begun for all the cadets, and it was Christmas Eve Day. She had dreaded this holiday, but with Bernard to hang out with, it brightened her prospects.

Unless Bernard wasn't the gift giver.

But who else could it be?

She rose and dressed for chapel and headed out the door to meet Bernard.

"Mornin'," he greeted.

"Merry Christmas, you mean." She gave him a big smile. "Sleep well?"

"Like a baby. Oh, wait. Babies wake a lot and cry at night, don't they?"

"It's been a long time since I've been one so I'm not 100 percent sure. I suspect you're correct."

They arrived at the post chapel, which was sparsely attended, again due to so many being on leave. Still, it was where she needed to be for now. Right here, in this moment, in this place, with this man.

The traditional Christmas songs warmed her soul, and instead of experiencing the loneliness she'd anticipated, her heart was full of the wonder and joy of the amazing gift God had given in His Son, Jesus.

Yanks flitted across her mind. The man was lost without Jesus and hadn't been able to respect her wishes. He'd had plenty of opportunities to get the message. What if it had been a cadet without as much steel? He could have injured that woman…or worse. She couldn't regret her actions. He was reaping the reward for his misbehavior. Sin came home to roost for Yanks and God graciously protected her from far worse. She tugged at her sleeve to find the bruise he'd left behind. She covered it before Bernard could notice.

Worship ended and the chaplain gave a sweet message. She was glad there was also a candlelight service this evening. There wouldn't be many people there, but it would be good. Like doing the laundry, she needed to keep her focus positive.

Service ended, and they walked over to the dining facility. There was a limited selection as many of the food servers were also on leave for the holiday. Tomorrow they would have a big meal for those remaining. They went through the line, got their food, and sat down across from each other.

"Since it's just the two of us, would you mind if I prayed?" Bernard asked.

"No. Go right ahead." She bowed her head and let his prayer wash over her.

"Lord, thank You for keeping Brooke safe last night and for giving us friendship and company for this holiday celebrating Your birth. Thank You for this food and the opportunity to worship You."

"Amen," Brooke said. She raised her head and gave Bernard a smile. What would it be like to be led by a man like this at home as well as at work? He'd always been honorable and kind. A great working companion. Wishful thinking.

"Wanna take a run later this morning, before lunch?" Bernard asked.

"Yes, as a matter of fact, I would."

A running partner to boot. Thank You, Lord.

Bernard returned to his room and paced. His roommates were gone and would not return for a week. He was sure he'd be keeping busy during that time. Tomorrow he planned a video chat with his mom and sisters. Dad was overseas and unavailable. He hoped they all liked the gifts he'd selected for them. Thankfully, during his last two years in school he'd been doing some teaching while he finished his degree and received a decent stipend from that. He'd been living frugally, if working, teaching, studying, living on coffee, and occasionally getting a nap, counted for living. It was what had allowed him to get the gifts for Brooke. He was grateful his aunt was stationed at Fort Benning and worked close and had access to the barracks. She'd been more than happy to help him out. She'd leave the last gift today before heading out to spend time with her family. He was sure the *how* of the gifts was annoying Brooke as much as the *who*.

She was a woman with a plan and liked to understand things completely. This mystery must be annoying her, yet she didn't say anything. He admired her being circumspect. Of course, her roommates would spill when another gift had come in and all of Bravo Company was aware. He wondered if that's why Yanks turned his focus on her. Someone was interested and that drew him like a red cape to a bull. Yanks was probably compelled to charge and check it out.

Little did the man realize that the bull had skills.

Even yesterday, Brooke never mentioned the gifts and poems. Haugh and Xavier indicated she was thrilled with the gifts, and they swooned while sharing with someone else where he overheard. Eavesdropping wasn't a crime, and he hadn't sought out the information. It comforted him to learn that she'd appreciated the gifts so far and that they'd been received with such warmth. Of course, all the other women in Bravo Company were curious and jealous at the same time.

Which also meant they would all discover he was the giver after Brooke did. There's no way that could be kept secret. What had he been thinking? He'd been careful. It was as if he put his adoration for her in a lockbox when he left his room to go about his day as a cadet. Treat her the same as every other cadet. Corsin suspected his feelings ran deeper. VanderLoo entertained the thought that maybe he'd have a chance after graduation.

Had Bernard been wise in sharing his heart this way to win the woman of his dreams? Or had it been foolish? Would she even accept the final gift? If anything, she'd be kind in rejecting him. She wouldn't be cruel or embarrass him. She hadn't even done that to Yanks. The man did that to himself by overstepping his bounds. Had Yanks pushed too far with other female cadets who'd been too afraid to report it? Possibly. Women needed to work hard to earn the respect of some men. Brooke had his respect way back in high school.

Time would tell how this all shook out. He paced. They'd be going for a run soon, and enjoy lunch after that. This evening was his opportunity to end his misery…or deepen it. This could be a wonderful Christmas Eve filled with hope and promise—or the death of a dream.

Brooke collapsed onto her bunk and with her hands behind her neck she stared at the ceiling. It was a strange thing to be doing nothing after months of almost nonstop marching, learning, running, saluting, sweating, hurting, and not getting any sleep. Even today, the day of all days, she couldn't escape the realization that if her original plans had worked, she'd be on leave, getting married to Clay today, and returning to the barracks a week later.

Instead, she was here with seven weeks to go. Alone.

Clay was marrying someone else.

The fact that he chose to do that today could have made the loss more painful. As if he was trying to stab her, kill her hopes, or any love, as he twisted the knife in her gut. Instead, there was a brief pang of loss that had been replaced by hope of a better future without him.

She sat and pulled out the Christmas cards she'd received over the last nine days. She reread every one of them. She picked up the nutcracker and traced the minute detail of the painted and intricate wood design, while she admired the workmanship.

She was God's workmanship. She was in process. Losing Clay was a part of that in a good way. The wood this figure was carved from was beautiful because of what had been removed, not by what had been added. The pieces had been hewn out with precision and sanded with care. Was that what God was doing? He needed to strip away the unnecessary.

She enjoyed time spent with Bernard. Her heart ached with that old familiar longing she'd had as a sophomore admiring him as a senior. She wished she had her yearbook right now. To find that one photo where they were together in the choir of a musical, *White Christmas*.

Her first gift.

Last night's movie. Had Bernard orchestrated that? How would a cadet have that kind of influence?

Was he the giver of the gifts? If he were, what would be next?

What if he wasn't?

She sat the nutcracker back in his place of honor. God needed to strip away the old Brooke to make her a better officer and a kinder person.

Would He give her even more?

She changed for their run and headed out the door.

Bernard stretched as he waited for Brooke to leave the barracks. How many other cadets wanted to go running on Christmas Eve? Those who left post would be eating well and enjoying sleeping in and would return several pounds heavier and struggle to do what was now at least manageable even if it was challenging.

Not Brooke. She wanted to stay disciplined, and he admired her even more for that. Having a week of morning workouts together with no one else around would be bliss.

Unless she rejected him. Even then he'd still do it to be near her.

Was this how God loved? The Lord gave gift after gift in the covenants He'd offered to Israel, culminating in the best gift of all, God as the Son, Jesus. They shunned them repeatedly…but God the Father, Son, and Holy Spirit kept loving. All God wanted was for His people to accept His gift, freely given. He didn't need perfection or duty like the military did. He wanted hearts offered without reservation.

The weight of that caused Bernard to pause. Even when Jesus was rejected and scorned, He still loved. Every time the Israelites broke covenant, God remained faithful. All He wanted was their hearts. God wanted them to seek Him, worship, adore, and surrender to His will. Why did humans make it difficult? God gave everything. Every breath. He sustained life. He had a perfect and good plan for every one of His children if they followed Him. He never said it would be easy, but the rewards would be great.

Winning Brooke's heart might not be easy either. He'd stay faithful unless or until God made it clear she was not the woman for him.

Bernard hoped she was. He couldn't imagine a better partner for the life ahead. He couldn't envision any future worthwhile without her in it, by his side, returning his love.

And he had no control over that. Brooke possessed a strong will. She was fiercely independent. She did not waver in her confidence in God and herself.

Which meant that if she returned his affections—it would be a free and wonderful gift. A miracle.

God, please?

12

Brooke returned to the barracks after lunch with Bernard. The man had stamina and a cheerful attitude. They had fun making up silly cadences as they'd ran.

There was a girl her name is Brooke
One cadet dared take a look
She liked to run both night and day
That cadet couldn't stay away
When he tried to make her his own
She flipped him ov'r sent him home

Then Brooke made her own:

A stupid cadet named Yanks had met
A girl he couldn't seem to get
He tried so hard he broke a toe
So back home he had to go
Go, go, go he had to go
Go, go, go he had to go

She grinned as they chuckled and then recited some of the more common ones. Opening the door to her room she found an envelope that someone slid under the door with the same penmanship as the others, addressed to Officer Candidate Cooper-Sanchez.

Brooke set it down and proceeded to remove her coat and boots. She wanted to take a shower but didn't need to hurry; there was plenty of time. She picked up the envelope and settled on her bunk to open it. Same card as all the others. There was still a poem.

One last gift to reveal myself
In hopes you'll see me true
No pressure to reciprocate
Because of my affection for you.
You'll get this later by my own hand,
Please do not reject my plea
That you would be my Christmas love,
From now until eternity.

Wow. So, this was it. Today? Someone was going to reveal themselves as the giver of these gifts. And there was one more left come. She hoped it wasn't a ring. She hadn't discovered the identity of the gift-giver yet. Was she ready to have the truth revealed? If it wasn't Bernard, then who? There were no other men whom she regarded so highly, and it couldn't be anyone enlisted or even an instructor as that wasn't allowed.

Whew. She'd need to be praying about this, she wanted to be ready for whatever was to come. After all, that's what the Army was training her for. She suspected she'd need God's help with this more than her military training. The military didn't instruct in matters of the heart.

Returning to her room after her shower she dried her hair and settled back on her bunk. She pulled out her phone, a device that had sat, turned off, in her drawer. She dialed her sister.

Kobbe answered. "Brooke? I thought were going to video chat later with Mom, Dad, and Riley? Is everything OK?"

"Why, did you sense something was wrong?"

"You realize I can't pay much attention to that hypersensitive twin thing given the torture you're going through in OCS. You have been on my mind today, though. Something happened."

Brooke filled her in on the gifts, poems, what happened last night with Yanks, and then the last card.

"Whoever this is, you'd better be nice to him. He went through a lot of work. Not just getting you such great gifts but writing ten poems? I will assure you; it isn't me. And no one has sought me out to plumb the depths of who the genuine Samantha Brooke Cooper-Sanchez is and what she likes. I'd totally forgotten you loved Shakespeare's poetry.

I hated those classes. And *White Christmas?* Wow. It's been years since we've pulled out those makeshift fans to sing 'Sisters' together."

"Much less decorate a tree and sip chai."

"Exactly. Whoever is doing this is into you 100 percent. Even if it is a ring—you'd better be saying yes."

"What if it's someone I don't like in real life?" Brooke protested.

"At least give him a chance. Seek God. Pray about it. Write in that amazing journal, and you'd better be willing to report who it is when we're on that video call tonight."

"Fine. What's going on in your world that you might not be wanting to share with Mom and Dad. Any guys on your radar?"

After Brooke spoke with her sister for some time, they disconnected with "Merry Christmas" in unison.

She settled back down, turning her phone off and putting it away. She realized they never mentioned Clay once during their conversation. In her mind, that was progress. She did what her sister suggested and wrote all about it in her journal.

Bernard showered, prayed, paced, and struggled to wait till it was time to meet Brooke for dinner before chapel. When was he going to make his move? How? He didn't want anything public. God, please help a guy out here!

Finally, it was time, and he left his barracks to go stand outside and wait for Brooke to join him for a meal at the dining facility. When she emerged from the building his pulse accelerated. She smiled at him as she stepped alongside for the walk.

"It's weird doing this without a lot of people walking, marching, or running in step," she said.

"Do you want me to call a cadence from earlier or make a new one up?"

She chuckled. "No, it's a beautiful evening, with a little bit of snow on the ground that should be gone by tomorrow. There's a quietness without the crowds. Peace."

"I agree." Lord, please give me peace.

They entered the dining hall with Bernard holding the door for her to go first.

"Always the gentleman. Thank you."

"My pleasure."

They got their food and settled down. It was an odd thing to have so few people there.

"Can I pray for our meal?" he asked.

"Please."

Bernard bowed his head. "Lord, tonight we celebrate the greatest gift of all, Your Son, Jesus, a perfect and good gift for all who choose to accept Him. Open hearts to Your wonder and truth tonight as we celebrate Christmas. Thank You for this food and for time with Brooke. Amen."

"I called my sister this afternoon. We're doing a family video call later. Dad is in South Korea, as you know, it's already Christmas there."

"Kobbe is her name, right?"

"I'm impressed you remember."

"You two were quite the pair in high school. You both stood out but in different ways. Kobbe is a unique name and after an Army post. I guess you're both glad you're not named something like Benlux…"

"Darby wouldn't have been bad, but Bezmer?" Brooke said.

"Stanley, Buchanan, or if they stuck to the States: Irwin, Wainwright, Huachuca…"

"Dix, Benning, Gordon, Gillem. Could you imagine me as a Shelby?"

Bernard chuckled. "I admire your parent's dedication to the Army in the way they named their daughters. When I have kids, I hope my wife isn't so inclined. I'm not opposed if a name stuck out as great, but I don't want an Irwin, Stanley, or Bondsteel for a son's name."

"I understand. I doubt I'd want that either, but it was one of their quirks that they chose to do that, and I can't fault them for it. Kobbe's had a harder time, I think. Brooke has become a more mainstream name, so it's not as unique. Although we could have always chosen to go by our first names: Samantha and Victoria."

"Those don't fit. Kobbe likes to blend in more, right? Her name is more unusual." Bernard sipped his water.

"I'm not fond of standing out either but do tend to be a bit more outgoing. She has her strengths."

"My parents chose all names that began with a *B*. Betsy, me, and my sister Belle, and then Beatrix."

"I remember Beatrix, she was in my grade. Betsy must have already graduated. I don't remember Belle."

Bernard sighed. "She was thirteen when she tried to kill herself."

Brooke moved her hand across the table to cover his. "I'm so sorry. I wasn't aware. It was just an attempt?"

He shook his head. "She succeeded. It took a little longer, which was a torture of its own."

"How old were you?"

"Thirteen. Same as Belle. We were twins."

Brooke sat back, her hand pulling away. "I can't imagine how difficult that must have been for you. Especially being twins. Care to talk about it? What happened?"

Bernard sighed. "I don't like to talk about it, but Belle struggled with depression, and my father wouldn't take that seriously. Said she was seeking attention and insisted that Mother not take her to be evaluated. I even begged him to allow it and got smacked for it. He might be a good drill sergeant, but he was a harsh father."

"I'm so sorry." She placed a hand on his arm and the warmth of that gesture gave him the courage to continue.

"Belle made an attempt and I found her. My dad was overseas at the time. She was on life-support and my mom, myself, and my sisters were there when they had to finally pull the plug. Mom fell apart."

Brooke wiped a tear away. "That had to be so hard. Is that why you chose psychiatry as your specialty?"

"Yes. I wish I'd been wise enough then to see how much she was hurting. It never dawned on me that someone would do that. I was pretty naïve. Maybe because we're not identical, our brain chemistry was different? We didn't share that deeper connection some twins do.

85

My mom's depression was brutal, but she got help and survived. We all struggled with Belle's death. Sometimes I wonder if it's something I'll ever truly recover from. Part of me hopes not."

"While a horrific experience, from that will come the empathy that will resonate with your patients. How does your dad feel about your specialty?"

Bernard scoffed. "He doesn't think it's macho enough, but it's what I believe God has called me to. I learned long ago I needed to forgive my father, and whether he approves or not I need to follow God's leading in my life."

"It's an admirable choice, and I'm sure you'll be able to help many hurting people. The world is short on people in that profession. Sounds like things still aren't great with your father? I can't imagine how that must hurt. My dad's always been amazing and supportive."

"Yeah, well, when Belle died, I might as well have been gone too. I'm not sure if it was grief or just not being able to accept depression as anything other than a failure made him come down hard on all of us. I learned to stay under the radar as much as possible to avoid his censure. Didn't help.

"When you mentioned joining the national guard and the Army, that was all I needed to propel me on my own path. I admired your determination and then realized it might be a good path for me as well, whether my father approved or not. And now, here we are. It's like God was at work through it all. Enough about me though, let's talk about more cheerful things."

They did. They finished their meal and headed to chapel. They found an empty pew and sat.

Having Brooke by his side, understanding his deepest pain and offering him comfort, gave him hope...and a deeper certainty that she was the one God wanted him to spend the rest of his life with.

13

The candles were lit as the service came to an end and everyone singing "Silent Night" acapella warmed her heart. Brooke wasn't home with family, but the military had been her family too. Bernard standing by her side, an inch or two taller than her, gave her comfort. And hope.

Her heart ached for the loss of his sister. Lord, give him healing and peace. Thank You for bringing him here to Fort Benning to be a friend and confidant as we go through this. And thank You for saving me, for loving me, and for leading me. Happy birthday, Jesus.

People were moving to leave.

"Are you OK?" Bernard whispered.

"Yeah. Just praying. Kind of got lost in the moment." She blew out her candle. Bernard reached to take it and she gave it to him, making sure not to tip it to prevent the wax from dripping on the carpet.

"I understand how that can happen. Hope it never occurs when an instructor is about to call on me and finds I'm not paying attention."

Brooke chuckled.

They moved out from the seats to the back of the room where there were sugar cookies and hot chocolate. They grabbed one of each. Walking out to the hallway, they sat down in an alcove. Most cadets were rushing back to their quarters.

"I'm glad I got to share today with you. It's hard to be lonely when you're with a friend," Brooke said.

Bernard choked. "Inhaled a cookie crumb," he muttered as he

sipped some of his hot chocolate.

They sat in silence for a few moments as more people left.

"Brooke, I wanted to thank you for being such a good friend." He pulled a small wrapped box out of his pocket. "Merry Christmas."

"You got me a Christmas present? I didn't get you anything." She paused and took the box. It had been him. "Thank you."

"You haven't even opened it yet."

"I received nine other gifts I need to express my gratitude for, don't I? It was you all along?"

His face grew red, and he struggled to meet her gaze. "Yeah. I hope that's OK and you're not disappointed."

"I prayed hard it wasn't Yanks, Corsin, or VanderLoo." She grinned.

"Go ahead, open it," he insisted.

She set her empty cup down and opened the small box. Her hands shook. What did this all mean? She found a velvety rectangular clam box and opened it. Inside was the most exquisite cross, it was crafted silver and gold with a small emerald at the center with a silver box chain.

"Oh, Bernard. This is beautiful."

"Not as beautiful as you. I need to confess. I was half in love with you in high school but couldn't bring myself to ask you out. Every time we met for prayer around the high school flagpole, I wanted to tell you how I felt. Then when we saw each other again in college, you were dating someone else. I'm sorry Clay—"

She pressed a finger to his lips. "I don't want to talk about him. God needed me to be free from him to be here during this time, in this OCS, in this squad, platoon, and company to show me that He had someone so much better in mind for me. Your gifts and poems showed me that you had been paying attention for a long time. I was afraid to hope they were from you. You gave no indication that it was you, and it scared me that it wouldn't be." She took the necklace out and unfastened it. "Can you put this on for me?"

Bernard did and the touch of his fingers on her skin gave her delightful shivers.

She displayed it for now. He understood that religious jewelry could not be worn under her ACUs, the Army's latest change in the combat uniform, with black and coyote brown camouflage. Clay would have never gotten that or even considered it. There was a lot this man understood that no other man would.

Relief washed over Bernard at Brooke's gracious acceptance and appreciation for this gift and all the others. He still had one more thing.

"Shall we head back?"

She nodded. They donned their coats and started the walk to the barracks.

"I was worried you wouldn't be happy about it being me."

"Why?"

"Because you're kind to everyone. Not just me. I think half the cadets want to date you. Yanks had me worried the most for a while there."

"You realize now how unfounded those concerns were?"

"Yes. Your cadence this morning made that abundantly clear."

She chuckled.

He steered them behind a building.

"What…?"

"Shhh," Bernard said. He turned to face her, with a sliver of moonlight to guide him. "I have a question."

"OK?"

"Would it be all right if I kissed you?" he whispered as his head came closer to hers.

"Only if I get to kiss you back."

Her wide eyes and gentle smile caused hope to take flight within him.

Their lips met and he savored the kiss and the slight taste of sugar and chocolate. He pulled back to gaze into her eyes.

"Wow," Brooke said.

"Whew. I've never had a kiss like that before," he confessed.

"Me neither. Kiss me again?"

"Gladly."

When they finished that kiss, she leaned her head against his chest.

"We can't keep doing this," she said.

"I know. Rules. No PDA. We'll need to go on as we were before. You are now and always were the one who has my whole heart."

"And you have mine."

They walked back to the barracks. The next month and a half would be hard, but after that, he'd be able to hold her hand and enjoy more of those kisses. She was worth the wait.

If Brooke could float that would be how she got back to her room. She entered and shut the door. She clutched the nutcracker and held it tight. Bernard was hers. He had been the one who wooed her with stealth and anonymity. She wanted to squeal out of the joy that welled up within her. She hadn't lied about those kisses. None of the kisses she shared with Clay had the kind of potency combined to match even one of Bernard's.

She checked the clock. It was time for the video chat with her family. She had so much to share—and much more she couldn't. She pulled out her phone and texted Kobbe.

It was Bernard. He has my heart.

You kissed?

Don't tell Mom and Dad.

I can keep a secret.

She logged on to the video chat. "Merry Christmas!"

Brooke's heart was full and even though she wanted to keep their romance a secret for now. There was something sacred about the connection they had that was too fragile to talk about yet. In time she'd tell them. But for now, she held it close to her heart. If anyone was worth waiting for, Bernard was.

Epilogue

February
Commissioning Day

Brooke tucked her cross necklace under her uniform. This was it. After today she and Bernard could date. Letters, speaking glances, and stolen kisses were all well and good, but it wasn't enough for Brooke. She suspected Bernard was ready for the hiding to be over as well.

The cadets were ready to complete their final task. Graduation ceremony. The freezing weather forced a change of plans from an outdoor event to an indoor ceremony. Xavier echoed Brooke's sigh of relief when they found out they wouldn't be standing in formation for two hours enduring the cold while each of the distinguished speakers spoke at great length.

The cadets wore their Class Bs, their Army green service uniform looking sharp and stood in the same assigned positions they had since the first day. Facing forward. Eyes straight. Hands behind their backs with their feet shoulder width apart. No speaking or movement of any kind. All of them waiting in Epson Hall for their name to be called to receive their OCS diploma.

"Attention." The entire class of thirty snapped from their parade rest posture to attention as one movement.

"Welcome, General Hendricks, Mayor Jolley, family, and friends. OCS cadets, today you will become the officers you've trained to be.

From this day you will put into practice the leadership skills you learned over the last few months," Commandant Weibe said.

Wow. It's done. Thank You, Lord, for always going before me and showing me the path You have for me. Thank You for the wonderful surprise of Mom, Dad, and Riley showing up today. Lord, You are the Giver of good gifts. Thanks. Brooke tuned out the lengthy speeches to have her chat with God.

Bernard stood at attention with more enthusiasm than the occasion called for, but his plan to talk to Billy Cooper and ask for Brooke's hand in marriage was burning a hole into his gut. What if he says no? Bernard's thoughts whirled around in his head; he almost missed his name being called.

"Second Lieutenant Bernard Travis."

He moved toward the stage and up the four steps to receive his diploma from the commandant who smiled as he reached out to shake Bernard's hand.

"Officers, you may celebrate with your family and friends in the reception center next door. Class dismissed."

The cadets dispersed to find their loved ones. Bernard's family didn't come to the graduation, but the Coopers had surprised Brooke and were all there, including Brooke's twin sister, Kobbe.

He strode over to Brooke's family just as she was enveloped into a group hug. There was lots of laughter and talking at once.

Bernard cleared his throat. "Mr. Cooper? Can I meet with you sometime yet today?"

Billy nodded his head. "Hey, St. Bernard! I remember you. Congratulations! Sure, son. Come to the hotel and I'll meet you down in the lobby. The women always take a little longer to get ready."

"Great. Thank you. I'll be there." Bernard gave a nod and headed back to his room. He had some praying to do before tonight.

Bernard's hands were sweating although the temperature was below freezing. He walked over to the guest sign-in area and met what he hoped would be his future father-in-law.

"Bernard, how are ya?" Billy Cooper asked.

"Relieved OCS is over, and we can move on to our assignments. Brooke told me you transferred to Rucker a few weeks ago. How are things there? Anything new at the schoolhouse?"

"Nope. Same old stuff. Lots of flying and waiting." Billy chuckled. The two men sat down in a nearby alcove with several chairs and a television.

"Sir, I'd like to ask you something." Bernard tried to remember to sit up straight, eyes focused on Billy, striving to keep his voice strong.

"Sure. What's going on?"

Bernard's hands began to sweat and his left knee began bouncing. "Well, sir. I've been in love with your daughter—" Bernard wasn't able to finish because Billy interrupted him.

"What? Which one? Kobbe, Riley, or Brooke?" Billy struggled to suppress his grin.

"Oh no, sir. Brooke, sir."

"Brooke, huh?" The man's voice carried a serious weight to it.

"Umm, I've been in love with Brooke since high school and want to ask her to marry me. Would you give us your blessing?"

Billy wrapped Bernard in a big bear hug while slapping him on the back. "Of course. Son, I guessed you were in love with her back then, and I'm tickled pink to have you as my son-in-law. Yes. You absolutely have mine and her mom's blessings."

The Cooper family changed clothes before dinner. Brooke was sharing a room at the hotel with her sister Kobbe who was going with the rest of the family.

"How do I look?" Brooke asked.

Brooke's black winter dress jacket hung open to reveal a black velvety top and green skirt. Her cross necklace rested visible for all to see. The emerald green scarf was tucked under the collar of the coat and the mittens were held in her hand.

"You are going to knock his socks off, sis. You're gorgeous." Kobbe gave her sister a hug. "We'll meet you at the restaurant." She grabbed her coat and left.

Brooke took one last glance in the mirror and gently touched the cross. What would be next for Bernard and her? God, let me be ready for whatever You have planned next. It was hard to give up control of life to God, but she'd done it with the military, she could do it with God...and perhaps be better as a girlfriend. Or someday, something more. Somehow with Bernard it all seemed possible and wonderful. Stop dreaming. He's waiting for you!

She took the elevator down and spied Bernard in the lobby. His eyes brightened when he saw her and that smile made her stomach do flip flops. She grinned at him. They held hands as they walked outside.

"You're gorgeous." Bernard helped her into the vehicle he'd rented. "I have a slight detour before we join your family for dinner. I hope you don't mind."

"I'm hungry, but if I can have kisses as an appetizer I might be agreeable to that detour."

He chuckled. "I might be willing to accommodate my lady's wish." He drove to Building One and parked near the post flagpole. He turned to her. "Come, walk with me."

She gave him a curious glance. "OK, it is a bit chilly out."

"This won't take long."

Bernard rushed around to her side of the vehicle, opened the door and offered his hand. She was breathtaking dressed in civies and heels.

Stop drooling.

They walked a short distance to a bench that overlooked a pond where a few swans floated, and the flagpole was illuminated.

"It's lovely here at night. This reminds me of when we would meet and pray at the flagpole before school," Brooke said as she stepped over to the wooden bench.

He sat by her side. "I hoped you would remember that time too. I am proud of you, Brooke. I have longed and prayed for this day. In high school I often prayed beside you for this day to happen."

He got off the bench and dropped to one knee. Breathe man, you can do this.

"Bernard?" Brooke asked.

He reached for her hands with his. "You have been my heart's desire from the day we first met. Since then, my love's grown deeper still, every time we've met. You are the one God has given, if I am hearing Him clear, so please say yes to marrying me, for I love you, my dear."

He removed one hand and dug in his pocket and lifted a ring up to her. "Would you put me out of my misery and allow me the honor of loving and cherishing you for the rest of our lives together?"

"Yes. Yes. And yes!" She leaned forward and touched both sides of his head. "I love you, Bernard Travis, and I would be delighted and honored to be your wife under one condition."

He frowned. "What is it?"

"That you never withhold your kisses from me—"

"Unless we're in uniform in public," they said in unison.

"Done," he said.

"Then get on with it," she smiled as she brought her lips to his.

All the magic of Christmas Eve flooded in on him once again. He pulled them both to their feet. She put her left hand out and he slid the ring on.

"It matches my necklace."

The silver and gold with a modest emerald and two smaller diamonds fit well. "A beautiful ring for a beautiful woman."

"Let's go share our good news," Brooke said.

"Not until you kiss me again," Bernard insisted.

"You don't need to ask twice."

"I didn't ask." Bernard said in a low voice.

And once again the kiss caused his heart to somersault.

She let him go and they were both breathless. "How soon can we make this wedding happen?"

"As soon as you wish." Bernard grinned. "Now, let's go share the news with your family."

"I'll go anywhere as long as it's with you." She reached to squeeze his hand.

"Ditto. I love you, Brooke."

"Love you, too, my Lieutenant Bernard Travis."

Enjoy a preview of
Operation Allegiance, Book 2
of the Rules of Engagement Military Romance Series.

Prologue

The bottle rockets soared high into the air above the surrounding Rocky Mountain peaks, bathing the mountains in a colorful glow. Alexandros laughed. "Rusty. Did you see that one?" His brother's grin was evident in the fading moonlight.

"Yeah! I'm surprised no one from the camp has discovered us missing. Alexos, you rocked it coming up with this idea."

Alexandros, known as Alexos to many of his family and friends, nodded. "It was hard not rolling my eyes at Dad this afternoon when he lectured me, again, on being *responsible* this summer at camp. And in front of all our friends and youth group, too."

"I almost bust a gut trying to stop from laughing. He means well though. It's weird to think it's our last summer here. Next year we graduate and will have to put this all behind us." Rusty groaned as he lit another bottle rocket and the teenagers stepped back from the cliff edge, hands over their ears at the deafening scream as it soared high overhead and exploded in the air. The sound was amplified by the surrounding mountains.

"Woop!" Alexos yelled. "Says you. I don't plan on putting any of this fun behind me."

"Me either. Wait till you see this one." Russ pulled a huge thick stick out of his bag. His curly head bobbed with excitement.

"Wha—t? Where did you get that?" Alexos' chest clenched with alarm.

"I found it back in one of the old sheds. I bet she'll be a beauty."

"I don't think we—"

Russ already lit the fuse but hadn't stuck it into the ground.

Eyes wide and heart racing, Alexos screamed, "Toss it!"

Russ released the stick as it reached the end of the fuse. The explosion over the edge of the cliff blinded Alexos.

"Wow, bro. That was awesome. Hey…Rusty? Where are you?" His ears rang from the explosion. After that blast of light his eyes couldn't adjust. "Come on. This isn't funny. Tell me where you are."

Silence. A lone owl hooted in the distance and a coyote howled. The hair stood up on Alexandros' arm and goosebumps covered his entire body. An involuntary shiver overtook him as terror settled deep in his gut.

"Rusty?" he whispered.

He still couldn't find his brother. He went to the aspen tree where they had dropped their flashlights. He picked up his and turned it on. All he could see around him were trees, rocks, and underbrush. Alexos gulped. "Rusty?" Tears threatened at the corners of his eyes. If anything happened to his brother…

He crept to the edge where Russ had tossed the dynamite. He aimed the flashlight down and the reflective stripes on his brothers' jacket glowed. His brother's still body sprawled out on the rocky ground below the cliff.

Stifling a gasp, Alexos called out. "Rusty!" He waited for only a few seconds as the shout echoed off the surrounding mountains. His brother didn't answer. "I'm going to get help. Hang on, Russ. You're going to be all right."

He headed down the trail back to camp as fast as he could. *Lord, save my brother! Please!* Guilt tore at him, hurting more than the branches that ripped at his face and coat as he raced for help.

How was he ever going to face his father now?

The pilot and rescue workers teamed together to get Russell's body out of the canyon. A treacherous task in the dark. Alexos was in awe of what they'd accomplished. There was no way to know Rusty's condition, but he was alive.

Two hours after the initial explosion, Alexos watched from a distance as a rescue chopper airlifted his brother to the hospital. His tears had dried. Pastor Blake, also known to the students as PB, wrapped his arms around him. "Your parents are meeting us at the hospital. I'll drive you there."

Campers cleared a path in a *walk of shame*. PB led Alexos to the van they had arrived in earlier that afternoon. No one said a word. They didn't need to. He recognized the truth.

He was to blame.

1

Mandatory fun? Right? 0530 training at the Hump, in South Korea, outdoors…in November. Loads of fun. CW3 Alexandros Sava scoffed under his breath. He didn't think the old man had ever laughed a day in his life. Sweat trickled down his back even though he could see his breath in the twenty-eight-degree morning. The Black Cat's company commander made a wager that his pilots and crew would wipe the field with the medical unit from M.A.S.H. at Camp Humphreys. Alexandros wasn't going to be the one to disappoint a superior.

"Come on, chief, one more point and we got the win." Second Lieutenant Carlos Ortega meant well, but what did a butter bar know about anything?

Alexandros picked himself up and tested his aching ankle while knocking the dew-covered grass from his leg. He half-limped, half-jogged back to his team as they planned their next attack.

Once back in the game, yells of "Go Chief! Go Chief! Go long!" rang in his ears. Out of the corner of his eye, Alexos spotted Ortega jumping up and down on the sideline.

"The day they started letting infants become officers was the day the Army lost its dignity," CW3 Sava grumbled.

He took off running as fast as his sore ankle would allow. A soldier learned to push through pain. That was part of the training, and this *game* was much more than that. It was a workout and couldn't be avoided. The military didn't suffer wimps.

Corporal Yi was too quick for Alexandros' reflexes, slipping on the wet grass in front of him until it was too late. The shorter Korean soldier leapt for the frisbee at the same time, and they crashed to the ground together.

Alexandros screamed in pain. Was that really his voice?

Corporal Yi staggered to his feet and offered a hand to the larger officer. "Need some help, old man?" he wisecracked.

CW3 Sava groaned, unable to put his pain into words. The five-foot corporal bent over to help the six-foot-three-inch Alexandros to his feet.

Oh, this should be good. Not.

"You good, sir?" Corporal Yi asked, his brows suspiciously linking above his eyes.

Words he shouldn't be thinking threatened to slip past his lips as pain stabbed up his leg as he tried to move his ankle.

"You don't look too good, sir. I don't think your foot should go that way," Yi said.

Really? Nothing escaped Yi's keen eye. Where did they find this guy?

Two medics, who probably began shaving last week and were barely legal to drive, jogged over to assess him. They called for supplies and soon had his ankle and foot splinted. When did they stop giving you something to bite on when pain was this bad? His tongue barely avoided being bit as he tried to hold in the screams that sought release.

I'm sorry, Rusty. Did you suffer like this? The thought of his brother's pain racked with him guilt. His heart ached more than his leg. Halfway around the world and the past rose to taunt him once again. Alexos was grateful Rusty was alive but the sense of guilt never left him.

The medics were professional and soon helped him up on his one good leg. He nearly fell before the two young soldiers could get a better grip on him. He was hard to carry when he wasn't struggling against them and almost impossible to get him somewhere he didn't want to go. He was being difficult but couldn't help himself as they maneuvered him to their privately owned vehicle, or POV. He could barely fit in the tiny Korean car due to his height. Biting back the tears, he gritted his teeth and clutched the door handle tight to keep from making noise.

The specialist behind the wheel nodded to him. "That's real ugly, sir. The doc will probably send you to Young San to get that fixed."

"Are you kidding me?" he said through gritted teeth. "I'll shake it off. Just give me a minute." Bravado, pride, or was it wishful thinking? He'd never hurt this bad before. Walking it off was not going to be an option this time.

The news didn't get better after the doctor returned with X-rays. Lieutenant Colonel Maddox broke the bad news to Alexandros. "We won't be able to do what you need here. The day after tomorrow, we'll send you on to Tripler and from there Walter Reed for surgery. There's too much damage. You need an MRI before they can operate, and the swelling needs to go down. My staff is already making arrangements and your unit commander has been notified.

"I'll give you some sedatives to numb the pain. Your medevac is in one hour, so if you need something from your quarters, we can send someone to get it for you. You aren't going to be mobile for some time. Any questions?"

"Sir, will I be returning to Camp Humphreys?" Alexandros asked.

"It's highly doubtful. Your flying career may be over. With the damage you've done over the years and today's event, you'll likely have several surgeries and months of recovery. I'm sorry."

Alexandros gulped and nodded. "Thank you, sir." He replied to the officer the way he'd been trained. Some things never changed no matter what your rank or circumstances.

The sedatives did their job quickly and he slept through most of the flight on the C-5, waking an hour away from Tripler Army Medical Center.

"Welcome to Hawaii, Chief." A cheery voice roused him from a deep sleep.

His eyes cracked open to find a ray of sunshine piercing into his brain. He closed them tight and turned his head away. "Does it need to be so bright in here?" he grumbled. Cracking open his eyes again, he slowly took in the room, starting with the yellow ceiling before finally peering at his body. His leg was suspended by some contraption. "What in the world? What did you do to my leg?" he demanded, but not with as much strength as he had hoped for. He passed out before the nurse could answer.

Someone stroked Alexandros' chin. It was an odd sensation, equal parts calming and irritating. How long had it been since he'd shaved? He wanted to open his eyes but couldn't summon the energy. Who...?

When he awoke again the ceiling was different. Grey greeted him now. How depressing in the dimly lit room. Greek words were rapidly exchanged off to his left. His parents were here? Why? Was he dying?

He closed his eyes as his mom whispered prayers over him. The soft comforting cadence of her voice soothed him, much like when he was a little boy afraid of thunderstorms. At least once a month they communicated via video chat with them when he was overseas. Hadn't he talked to them a few days ago? He had no idea how much time had passed. If they were with him now, it must be serious. What happened? He wanted to tell her not to bother God with her prayers. It was a pointless exercise, but if it made her feel better...God certainly wasn't interested in his life.

He was tired. So tired.

He cracked open his eyes again to see his mother's greying head bent over folded hands. His father stood next to her, with one hand on her shoulder and the other touching Alexandros' arm. Their hair was greyer than he remembered. Alexos lifted his hand to touch his mom and let her know he was awake. Her olive skin was nearly the same color as his.

"Hey, *Mamá, Papá.*" His scratchy voice was soft.

"Oh, *agápi mou.*" A tear crept down her cheek as she reached to caress his face with her hand. His father stepped back to allow her to get closer, walking to the window to gaze outside.

Once again, he had disappointed his father. He was surprised they abandoned the ranch, church, and café to be here with him. Wherever *here* was.

"Alexandros, how do you feel?" His mother's eyes pled with him for good news.

"My leg hurts. Where am I?"

His father turned to face him but didn't come closer. "You're at Walter Reed." The voice was deep and dispassionate.

"What did the doctor say?" He was afraid to find out but given what he could see and that wiggling his big toe caused pain, he figured he hadn't lost his leg at least.

"You've had two surgeries. They are hopeful, but…" His mother glanced to her husband.

"But?" Alexos dreaded asking.

Arms folded across his chest, his father frowned. "They expect it will be several months for recovery."

Alexandros squeezed his eyes shut. They didn't know this had probably already ended his career. "It was just combat frisbee."

His mother shook her head. "We are grateful God has brought you back to us. It's an early Christmas miracle." She gave a soft grin as she tapped his nose with her finger. "Especially since you are in one piece…maybe with a few extra parts added."

"I hope no more screws fall loose in you, boy." His father cracked a small grin, a rare thing from his stern authoritarian dad. Peace filled Alexandros' soul. He couldn't wait to get home, recover, and prove the doctors wrong. He would fly a chopper again. He needed to. Without that—he was nothing.

Three months at Walter Reed and Alexos was still not ready to face the trip home to Colorado. It would be long and painful. His parents hadn't been able to remain long at Walter Reed Medical Center in Bethesda, Maryland, so his time there had been lonely and boring when the doctors weren't torturing him. The cute nurses weren't even a temptation. If he couldn't rejoin his unit, home was the next best place to be.

His mom met him when he landed at Colorado Springs Airport. The blonde female medic who accompanied him handed his mom a packet.

"What's that, Lieutenant?" he asked, weary from the trip, although he slept most of the way due to the sedative they gave him to make the journey easier to bear.

The nurse shook her head at him. "Chief Mr. Sava grumpy pants. I was only relaying the information from the doctor as to your care and medications and your follow up visits here in Colorado. Someone needs to kick your rear into gear, so you can become more mobile."

"Pretty sassy, aren't you?" he grumbled, as her comments hit too close to home. The fact that he needed a *keeper* and that it was his mom who was saddled with the task, humbled him.

"Alexandros. Apologize to the young lady," his mom chided.

"Sorry," he mumbled.

The young woman gave a smile. "Too bad I'm heading overseas after I return to Maryland. I wouldn't mind taking care of a handsome soldier like you once you got over yourself." She saluted with sass and left him with his mother.

He frowned at the nurse's departing figure. Before this accident, he wasn't in the market for a girlfriend. Not that he didn't like women. He liked them just fine. He only believed that the happiness of marriage was something beyond what God would ever allow him to enjoy. Why would He? Some sins were too big for a holy and just God to forgive.

"Come on, son." His mother plopped the packet in his lap, released the brakes on the wheelchair, and began to push him toward the parking lot. "Let's get you some good home cooking to strengthen you. I suspect you've lost some weight during your recovery. Time to reverse that so you can heal."

"Yes, Mother." What else could he say? He went from one program of rehabilitation to another. At least here with the Rocky Mountains all around, he could relax a little and eat his mom's homemade cooking.

There was no one to impress here. He was determined to recover. No one or nothing would stand in the way of his dream to fly again.

Once home, his father came to wheel him to the porch and handed him crutches. "They tell me you can manage these things. I've not had time to build a ramp, so let's see what you can do."

Pain meds were wearing off, but he had something to prove. He set the brakes on the wheelchair, grabbed the crutches, and hefted himself to his one good foot. With a grunt he worked himself away from the chair and one step at a time made it to the porch. How'd he get so weak so fast?

His father carried the wheelchair up and took it into the house. Alexandros followed as his mother held open the door.

"I suppose you didn't get an elevator to the second floor installed, so either I have to hobble up and down or sleep on the couch."

Mrs. Sava shook her head. "There is a daybed in the old room you and Rusty used before we added onto the house. You'll be able to sleep there. If you want a shower, however, you'll need to use the en suite in the master bedroom or tackle the stairs."

"Thanks, Mamá. I'm sure the daybed will be fine. Don't tell me you painted the room pink though."

She chuckled. "Go check for yourself. Dinner will be on in an hour so get some rest or unpack. Your next dose is later."

Alexandros shook his head. "Are you sure about that?"

"I have it in writing."

"You're not forgetting that Maryland is two hours ahead of Colorado, are you? I could have sworn it was time for that med before I ever left the airport." The screaming from his ankle was making that clear to him.

Pursing her lips, he watched her do the math in her head. "You're right. I'll bring you some water and your pill, but I'm not getting up in the middle of the night to do this for you. You'll need to adjust to mountain time. You're not in Maryland anymore."

He wasn't in South Korea either, where he belonged. He wondered how his unit was doing and hoped they were getting along without him and missing him all at the same time. He hobbled to the old bedroom he, Rusty, and his younger brother Kristos had shared until his parents built the house up a story to accommodate their expanding family.

Collapsing on the bed, he bit back a groan at the deep throbbing in his leg from the exertion. Alexos leaned up to take the pill his mother brought him and reclined to wait for the medication to kick in.

About the Authors

DeeDee Lake is The Connection Expert and lives in Colorado Springs with her amazing hubby of thirty-nine years, Seth, and two crazy dogs. Her golden-doodle, Bella Rose, can be found busting in when DeeDee is on Zoom, with the tiny Shi-Tzu following close behind.

DeeDee is a speaker, author of *Next Step. You've Accepted Jesus. Now What?*, blogger, columnist, relationship coach, part-time adult, potato fan, Navy brat, Army wife, type-A, and an extreme extrovert. She's lived in fifty houses and can pack up a house faster than an Olympic skier.

DeeDee believes relationships are built one conversation at a time.

She loves Jesus, her man, family, friends, and strangers. She's the owner of Cherish Relations Retreats and Workshops. DeeDee lives out her faith, guiding individuals how to experience extraordinary relationships.

If there is laughter and chatting, you can be sure she'll be there! Check out her blog at www.deedeelake.com or connect with her on facebook.com/DeeDeeLake.speaker.

Susan M. Baganz is happily married to Ben and is a native of Wisconsin. Susan writes adventurous historical and contemporary romances with a biblical worldview.

She speaks, teaches, and encourages others to follow God in being all He has created them to be. With her seminary degree in counseling psychology, a background in the field of mental health, and years serving in church ministry, she understands the complexities and pain of life as well as its craziness.

Her favorite pastimes are lazy…snuggling with her senior rescue dogs while reading a good book or sitting with a friend chatting over a cup of spiced chai latte, or more recently running the skid-loader to help with outdoor projects at home.

You can learn more by following her blog at susanbaganz.com, her Twitter feed @susanbaganz or her fan page, facebook.com/susanmbaganz.

Acknowledgments

DeeDee Lake would like to thank Susan M. Baganz Lodwick for a friendship that God surely created. Her love, encouragement, acceptance, and willingness to bring to life this manuscript that began thirty years ago means so much to me. Meeting at our first CCWC event set the tone for an amazing relationship. To say thank you to my precious husband, Seth, isn't enough. He believed in me when I was ready to stop the presses years ago. His enduring enthusiasm for this project encouraged me more than I can say. Seth continues to bring romance, fun, safety, and love every day of our thirty-nine years together. I appreciate all my family and friends who have cheered me on over the years. To my heavenly Father, who loved me before I knew Him, I owe Him my all. Every step of this military life You've gone before me and always had the perfect plan. Thank You, Lord!

Susan M. Baganz would like to thank DeeDee Lake for the love, laughter, and friendship that have brought about this partnership in spite of the miles that exist between Wisconsin and Colorado. Thanks to my hubby, Ben, for his faith and support of my writing career and for showing me what true love and dedication are like. Thanks to my friends: Heidi, Elisabeth, Kaye, Kerry, Beth, and so many more who have supported my writing. Thank you especially to God who saved me, redeemed my pain, and has called me to this opportunity to bless others and share the wonder and love of our amazing Lord Jesus. It is an honor and a privilege to be His talmidim. May all honor, glory, and praise be to Him.

More great books from…
CROSSRIVERMEDIA.COM

LOVE FINAL SUNRISE

New Yorker Ruth Jessup and Amish-bred Joshua Stutzman live in different worlds, but their lives collide as they battle wits against a psychopath and the New World Order. Suffering from amnesia, Ruth finds herself in a world without TVs, cell phones, or computers, only buggies and lanterns, planting and canning. If not for Joshua, Ruth would be lost and homeless. An attraction blossoms, but the chaos of the biblical seven-year tribulation blankets the world. Can Joshua's Amish ways help them survive the next three-and-a half years without the mark of the beast?

OBEDIENT UNTO DEATH

Sinister forces are at work to destroy the fledgling Christian faith in Ephesus, and Sabina is in their way. A young scribe is murdered during a covert Christian worship service. Sabina, a member of this outlawed religion, can't believe a member could be the killer. But when her Roman magistrate father arrests the church bishop for murder, she realizes all is not brotherly love among the faithful. Racing to stop the bishop's execution, Sabina scrambles for proof of his innocence. Will she discover the truth in time, or will she be thrown in prison herself for her faith in Christ?

SURVIVING CARMELITA

It was Josie's hands on the wheel, her foot on the pedal. Her fault. Now, sweet Carmelita will never see her fifth birthday. Where do you run when your world implodes and you can't function? Josie leaves her Chicago suburban home to stay with a cousin in Key West, unaware her journey is guided by an unseen hand. Unaware that a trailer park pastor, a battered horse, a pregnant teen, and a mysterious beachcomber might just set her on the path toward an inconceivable hope and redemption.

Bold faith starts here.

DIVINE DETOUR   WOOD

UNBEATEN   LINDSEY BELL

ABBA'S HEART   CLYMER

ABBA'S ANSWERS   BUTTERFIELD

ABBA'S LESSONS   LAKE

SURVIVING CARMELITA   MIURA

OBEDIENT UNTO DEATH   EYERLY

FORTUNES OF DEATH   EYERLY

ROOTS REDEEMED   SELLARS

Available in bookstores and from online retailers.

CROSSRIVERMEDIA.COM

If you enjoyed this book, will you consider sharing it with others?

- Please mention the book on Facebook, Instagram, Pinterest, or another social media site.

- Recommend this book to your small group, book club, and workplace.

- Head over to Facebook.com/CrossRiverMedia, 'Like' the page and post a comment as to what you enjoyed the most.

- Pick up a copy for someone you know who would be challenged or encouraged by this message.

- Write a review on your favorite ebook platform.

- To learn about our latest releases subscribe to our newsletter at CrossRiverMedia.com.

www.ingramcontent.com/pod-product-compliance
Lightning Source LLC
Chambersburg PA
CBHW061255170626
46809CB00007B/3002